"We're just about ready to begin the cheer-off," Coach Schultz announced. "We flipped a coin and Jessica Wakefield's squad will perform first. One more minute, girls, and then you're on!"

As they waited for their music to start, Jessica felt her heartbeat quicken in anticipation. A surge of adrenaline flooded her veins, and then the music began.

For a few minutes, Jessica wasn't aware of anything or anyone but the seven other girls she was performing with.

Her entire being was concentrated on the act of keeping in synch with her squad and performing her arm movements, footwork, and jumps with flair and precision.

The routine ended with each girl performing her most dramatic and polished jump combination and then they piled themselves into a pyramid. As Jessica and Lila boosted Jade to the top and then took their places at the side to support the girls at the bottom, the crowd leapt to its feet in a standing ovation.

The applause was thunderous. All eight girls fell on each other, hugging and laughing. "We did it!" Maria cried.

"Not a single mistake!" exclaimed Lila.

"There's no way Heather can beat that, no way," declared Jessica, her cheeks flushed with triumph. "We're going to regionals, you guys. I'm sure of it!"

THE POM-POM
WARS

Written by
Kate William

Created by
FRANCINE PASCAL

BANTAM BOOKS
NEW YORK · TORONTO · LONDON · SYDNEY · AUCKLAND

RL 6, age 12 and up

THE POM-POM WARS

A Bantam Book / February 1995

Sweet Valley High® *is a registered trademark of Francine Pascal*
Conceived by Francine Pascal
Produced by Daniel Weiss Associates, Inc.
33 West 17th Street
New York, NY 10011
Cover art by Bruce Emmett

ISBN: 0-553-56631-8

Published simultaneously in the United States and Canada

Bantam Books are published by Bantam Books, a division of Bantam
Doubleday Dell Publishing Group, Inc. Its trademark, consisting of the
words "Bantam Books" and the portrayal of a rooster, is Registered in
U.S. Patent and Trademark Office and in other countries. Marca
Registrada. Bantam Books, 1540 Broadway, New York, New York 10036.

PRINTED IN THE UNITED STATES OF AMERICA

OPM   0 9 8 7 6 5 4 3 2 1

To Jean and Burt Rubin

Chapter 1

Jessica Wakefield sat on the edge of her twin sister Elizabeth's neatly made bed, a clothbound notebook gripped in her hands. "I don't believe it," she said to herself, staring at the diary with wide, shocked eyes. "Liz and Ken—a hot and heavy fling—and I never even knew about it?"

The night before, hidden under Elizabeth's pillow, Jessica had found a small picture frame holding a strip of black-and-white photo-booth snapshots. Not terribly interesting, Jessica thought, until she realized that the boy Elizabeth was smooching with in the photos was Ken Matthews, not Elizabeth's longtime steady, Todd Wilkins! The same Ken Matthews who just so happened to be Jessica's new boyfriend.

The pictures weren't dated. Dying to know more, Jessica had taken the next opportunity to sneak into her sister's bedroom and search Elizabeth's diary for clues.

She'd expected a brief mention of Ken somewhere to explain the photo, along the lines of, "A bunch of us went out and Ken and I got silly in the photo booth. I've always had a crush on him, he's such a hunk, but of course he'd never be interested in me—he's more Jessica's type." Instead . . .

Propping a pillow against the headboard of Elizabeth's bed, Jessica leaned back and rested the diary against her tucked-up knees. Flipping back a few pages, she reread the first journal entry that related to Ken. Elizabeth had written it just a few weeks after Todd and his family moved from Sweet Valley, California, to Burlington, Vermont, leaving behind a—supposedly—heartbroken Elizabeth.

"Ken called me this afternoon, and we went to a movie tonight," recorded Elizabeth. "It almost seemed like a Saturday-night date, but of course he's just looking after me like Todd asked him to. Still, when we said good night, I was startled by the way I felt as I looked into his eyes. If I didn't know better, Diary, I'd think I was falling for Ken. . . ."

Jessica turned the page. "I can't give in to these feelings." Elizabeth had underlined the word "can't" about ten times. "He's Todd's best friend!"

But Elizabeth did give in, and this was where the diary really started to get juicy. Jessica scowled. It would be fun to read, if the boy Elizabeth was writing about was anyone but Ken . . . ! Half of her wanted to hurl the diary across the room; the other half couldn't tear her eyes from the page. She had to read each and every gory detail.

"I almost don't want to write this down,"

2

Elizabeth confessed. "I hope no one ever finds out about it. I can't believe I let myself get so carried away. . . ."

It made Jessica squirm to read her sister's swooning account of her first kiss with Ken. "We couldn't seem to stop touching each other, maybe because for weeks we'd been dying to do this, but holding back. Where will this end, Diary? There's no going back now. . . ."

On the next page Elizabeth was overcome with remorse. "Todd called. He doesn't seem to suspect anything. Why should he? I'm his girlfriend and Ken's his best buddy. If he can't trust us, who can he trust? I decided there was one surefire way to get rid of the guilt: Stay away from Ken. Who was I kidding? I might as well tell the ocean to stop crashing on the shore."

Jessica snorted. "'Tell the ocean to stop crashing on the shore'? Ugh, Liz, you are so corny. How did Ken stand it?"

Despite her disgust she kept reading, captivated by this tale of forbidden love. "We met at the beach again tonight," Elizabeth wrote. "I told my family I was going over to Olivia's to study for the French test. Diary, I've never felt so bad—and so good—at the same time. Ken kissed me like no one's ever kissed me before. . . ."

Jessica's blue-green eyes flashed with jealousy. How dare he kiss Elizabeth like that! Ken was supposed to be in love with her, Jessica. Had he really said outrageously mushy things to Elizabeth, like, "You're the sweetest, most beautiful girl I

3

know, I think about you every minute of the day, I adore you"?

"This was ages ago," Jessica reminded herself. "Liz and Ken momentarily lost their minds, that's all."

The affair seemed to go on forever, though. It had lasted only a few weeks, but Elizabeth spent pages and pages describing every secret rendezvous, every delicious stolen glance and kiss. Jessica pored over the diary, scandalized at the thought of her usually upright and honest sister doing so much lying and sneaking around. "I'm trying really hard to act normal around Ken at school so no one guesses what's going on between us. Luckily even Jessica doesn't seem to suspect anything, and she's got a nose for these things."

"Well!" Jessica declared indignantly. "Excuse me for not having such a devious mind that I could even imagine you'd be such a cheating two-timer!"

She dropped the diary on the bed and closed her eyes, suddenly feeling drained. First I quit the cheerleading squad, and now this. What a night!

The disturbing image of Elizabeth and Ken in a passionate embrace faded from Jessica's mind. It was replaced by an equally disturbing image from a key moment in that afternoon's football game against Claremont. Just as Jessica had been about to lead her squad into one of their standard school-spirit routines, her new cocaptain, Heather Mallone, had called out a cheer Jessica had never even heard of. While the other girls pranced and shouted, whirling and shaking their pom-poms and

4

dazzling the crowd with their fancy footwork, Jessica had just stood there with her own arms hanging limp at her side, looking and feeling like a total idiot. The home-team fans had leaped to their feet in thunderous approval; Jessica had hurled her pom-poms to the ground and stalked off the field, the two words she shouted—"I quit!"—completely drowned out by the applause for Heather's snappy new routine.

"The day that girl drove into town in her little white Mazda Miata was the worst day of my life," Jessica grumbled bitterly. From the start blond, beautiful Heather Mallone had been a thorn in Jessica's side. Head cheerleader at her old school, Heather had bulldozed her way onto the SVH squad just as Robin Wilson, formerly a cocaptain, announced that her family was moving to Denver. Jessica had proposed that she remain the squad's sole captain. Instead the other girls had voted unanimously: They wanted Heather as cocaptain.

She brainwashed them, pure and simple, Jessica thought glumly, remembering how Heather had shown up one day with cute new practice uniforms for the whole team. *Putting us all on that gross wheat-germ-and-broccoli "Cheer to Win" diet, and bragging constantly about how her old squad were the state champions for ten years in a row.* "Grr," she growled out loud. "Just thinking about it . . . !"

It had been bad enough when Heather had been just the new girl on the squad, showing off her great jumps and combinations every chance she got. When the squad had named her cocaptain, in Jessica's opinion at least, they had created a monster. The first thing Heather did, one day when Jessica was sick and couldn't make practice, was to kick Maria Santelli and Sandy Bacon off the squad. "We've got to trim the fat if we want to make it to regionals," Heather had declared coldly. Jessica was the only one who had protested Heather's high-handed decision; blinded by dreams of glory, the other girls had backed Heather a hundred percent. *And now Heather's gotten rid of me, too,* Jessica thought, punching Elizabeth's pillow. *She knew how I'd react when she pulled that stunt at the game today—she knew she'd drive me right over the edge!*

It burned her to a crisp to think that Heather Mallone had gotten the last word—or rather, the last cheer. "If I'm not a cheerleader, I'm nothing and nobody," Jessica mourned. "All I've got is Ken, and it turns out Liz had him first!"

Reaching for Elizabeth's diary, Jessica reread the last few entries about Ken. Apparently, the stress of secrecy had finally gotten to the pair, and after repeatedly trying to stay apart and then running back into one another's arms, they had finally managed to make the resolution stick.

"I did it," Elizabeth wrote on a page that was smudged and crinkled by teardrops. "After school Ken and I went for a walk in the park, and I broke things off with him. We got pretty choked up, but I know deep in our hearts we both understood it was the only thing to do. I'm lonely and he's lonely, so we just kind of naturally turned to each other, but

6

an actual out-in-the-open relationship would have been impossible and wrong. We could never have felt good about it. I think we'll be able to stay friends, though. There aren't any hard feelings. I'll always have a place for him in a secret part of my heart. And we promised each other: under no circumstances will we ever tell anyone about what happened between us. Never, ever."

Jessica closed the diary, a thoughtful expression on her face. One sentence of Elizabeth's in particular made a strong impression on her: "I'll always have a place for him in a secret part of my heart. . . ."

"That explains it," she deduced. "That's why Liz has been acting so weird lately and practically trying to talk me out of dating Ken. She's jealous!"

The realization gave Jessica a big emotional boost. It had definitely been unsettling to learn that her sister was once involved with Ken, but whatever had happened in the past, it was clear now that the only girl Ken got hot and bothered about was Jessica herself. *It must drive Liz crazy to see us together,* Jessica thought with a smug smile. *Serves her right!*

No, what was most interesting about Elizabeth's secret diary, Jessica decided, wasn't that Elizabeth had a fling with Ken Matthews. Jessica couldn't blame her sister for that—after all, Todd was three thousand miles away at the time, and Ken was the most adorable boy in Sweet Valley. No, it was that they'd managed to keep it a secret for all this time. *She never told me or Enid or anybody,* mused Jessica, *and I'm sure Ken didn't tell anyone, either.*

He certainly hasn't mentioned it to me! Which means Todd never found out that his supposedly devoted girlfriend cheated on him with his best friend.

Yes, that was very interesting, decided Jessica. Very interesting indeed!

"Poor Jessica," Elizabeth said to Todd as she dipped a tortilla chip into a bowl of spicy salsa. "Everyone's out celebrating the Gladiators' big victory, and she's sitting home alone!"

A party had spontaneously erupted at Winston Egbert's house, which was now packed with high-spirited Sweet Valley High football players, cheerleaders, and their friends. Standing by the refreshment table with Todd, Enid, Maria, and Sandy, Elizabeth glared across the room at the glamorous figure of Heather Mallone. "Jessica's sitting home by herself," Elizabeth repeated in a disgusted tone, "while Heather hogs all the glory."

"Talk about a guy magnet," said her best friend, Enid Rollins, tossing her auburn curls. "You'd think they'd be embarrassed to be seen drooling that way in public."

"It's not just the guys," Todd protested in defense of his gender. "Girls like her, too."

True, the crowd gathered around Heather was coed. "You're right," Elizabeth conceded, dipping another chip, "and that's the worst part. I can't believe Jessica's old cheerleading friends, especially Amy, aren't showing more loyalty to her. Instead, they're kissing up to Heather worse than ever!"

"They expect her to lead them straight to the cheerleading nationals," Maria Santelli reminded Elizabeth, "and I hate to say it, but I really think she can do it."

Elizabeth shook her head. "Maybe, but if you ask me, there are more important things than just winning competitions. I thought cheerleading was supposed to be about having a good time. Whatever happened to team spirit and good sportsmanship?"

"That's not Heather's philosophy," said Sandy with a sigh of resignation. "She's out to get what she wants, and if anyone stands in the way . . ." She drew her index finger across her throat to illustrate her point.

"Heather gave me and Sandy the boot because she thought we were holding back the squad," said Maria. "She had to find another way to get rid of Jessica, though."

"And now she has total control of the squad," concluded Sandy. "Talk about sly!"

Elizabeth poured herself a cup of soda, still fuming on her sister's behalf. Personally, she didn't see the attraction of cheerleading, but she knew it was important to Jessica; it was one of the few hobbies, besides shopping and boys, that her sister really got into body and soul.

Elizabeth remembered how happy Jessica had been the day the squad voted her cocaptain. *I didn't get it,* she admitted to herself. *How could anyone be that excited about something as silly as cheerleading?* In Elizabeth's opinion girls should have better things to do than hop around in short

9

skirts, cheering on the boys' teams. Of course, at Sweet Valley High the cheerleaders performed at both boys' and girls' games, but still . . . Jessica was such a great athlete—she could have easily made the tennis or softball or gymnastics teams. But no, it had to be cheerleading.

This difference in attitude was typical of the sixteen-year-old twin sisters. They were identical in appearance, with the same slim, athletic figures, honey-blond hair, turquoise eyes, and sun-warmed complexions, but no one who knew them well ever mixed them up . . . unless, that is, Elizabeth and Jessica wanted to be mixed up! They'd swapped identities on more than one occasion, but for the most part Elizabeth was happy to be the thoughtful, sensible, serious twin, and Jessica was happy to be the carefree, outrageous, irresponsible twin.

Of course, both girls knew that their personalities were more complex than that, but their reputations had a basis in truth. In addition to being a conscientious student, Elizabeth spent a good deal of her free time writing articles for the SVH newspaper, *The Oracle.* She finished her homework before making phone calls, and if she had a big test the next day, she resisted the temptation to blow off studying in favor of a movie or beach date with Todd. Jessica, on the other hand, reversed these priorities; her social life always came first. As for worrying about the future—college, a career—she was too busy enjoying the present!

I always thought I'd be psyched if Jessica quit cheerleading and put her energy into something more meaningful, Elizabeth reflected now, *but it shouldn't have happened like this. . . .*

"So you weren't able to talk Jess into coming to the party, either?"

Elizabeth blinked up at the speaker, startled from her reverie, and her cheeks flushed hot pink. Ken Matthews, the blond, well-built quarterback of the Sweet Valley High football team, and Jessica's current boyfriend, was smiling down at her. Jessica's current boyfriend . . . and once upon a time Elizabeth's secret love . . .

Elizabeth glanced quickly at Todd and was relieved to see he hadn't noted her telltale blush. "Uh, no. She said she didn't feel like talking to anybody, and she especially didn't want to run the risk of bumping into Heather."

As if on cue, Heather herself flounced up to the refreshment table. She was no longer in her cheerleading uniform, but the tight black dress she wore was just as short, revealing plenty of long, suntanned leg and quite a bit of shoulder and cleavage, too.

"Too bad about your sister," Heather said in passing to Elizabeth. "I guess she wasn't cut out to be a cheerleader. I'd say today's game separated the women from the girls, wouldn't you?"

Before Elizabeth could make a retort, Heather sashayed off with a cup of fruit punch. "The nerve of that girl!" she exclaimed.

"She's a monster," agreed Maria. "Poor Jessica never stood a chance."

Ken ran a hand through his bright-blond hair.

11

"I hate to see someone like Heather get the better of Jessica," he declared. "If only there were something I could do to cheer her up!"

"Just don't use the word 'cheer' around her," suggested Enid.

"There's gotta be something." Todd winked at Ken. "And if anyone can figure out what it is, it's you."

The others laughed. Elizabeth, meanwhile, felt as if the false smile she wore might crack her face in half. *I'm surprised they don't see right through me,* she thought. But, then, it wasn't always that hard to keep a big secret. She and Ken had successfully hidden their clandestine romance from the whole school—no one ever found out. *We wore masks,* she remembered. *We became actors, reading lines from a carefully crafted script.*

And now, after thinking that her relationship with Ken was over and done with, safely locked away in the past, Elizabeth found the old, confusing feelings crowding back to the surface. She watched Ken's face as he talked to Todd and Aaron and Bruce about a highlight of the football game. It was a handsome face, and an honest, open face . . . a face that, just a moment before, had been glowing with sincere concern and affection for Jessica. *He's not wearing a mask anymore,* Elizabeth thought. *I'm the only one who still has something to hide. . . .*

Safe in the knowledge that her sister would be out late, Jessica continued reading Elizabeth's diary. After breaking up with Ken, Elizabeth had started dating Jeffrey French. But then Todd's family moved back to Sweet Valley, and Elizabeth had to choose between Jeffrey and Todd. The diary was better than a romance novel!

When the phone rang, Jessica jumped guiltily, the diary flying from her hands. Leaping to her feet, she returned the notebook to its hiding place, then grabbed the receiver. "Hello?"

"Jess, it's me."

Despite her mood, Ken's deep, husky voice sent a happy shiver up Jessica's spine. "Hi, there."

"How are you feeling?" he asked, raising his voice in order to be heard over the noisy buzz of a party in the background.

"Still pretty crummy," she admitted.

"Well, I know you said you wanted to be left alone, but I have a proposition for you."

"What kind of proposition?"

"Meet me outside your house in ten minutes and you'll find out."

"Oh, come on. Tell me!" Jessica begged.

"Ten minutes, OK?" said Ken.

"It can't wait until tomorrow?"

"Nope, and I can't wait, either. I'm too nuts about you to waste a Saturday night apart!"

Jessica smiled. "When you put it that way . . . !"

Exactly ten minutes later Ken's white Toyota pulled up in front of the Wakefields' house on Calico Drive. Jessica was standing on the sidewalk, ready to hop into the passenger seat. "So, what's so urgent?" she asked him.

13

Ken gave her a swift kiss and then sat back again, smiling at her with sparkling eyes. "I've been thinking," he began eagerly, "about cheerleading."

"You've been thinking about cheerleading?" Jessica groaned. "Can we change the subject before I throw up?"

"I know you're depressed because you won't be cheering anymore, but this is the thing. There's no reason you have to stop doing what you like to do just because you're not on the squad anymore."

"Oh, really?" Jessica cocked an eyebrow. "Yes, I suppose you're right. I could cheerlead by myself in my backyard. Boy, that would be a riot," she said sarcastically. "Meanwhile, that bimbo Heather Mallone will be cheering with my squad in front of my school!"

"You don't need them," Ken persisted. "That's my point. You should start your own squad!"

"Start my own squad?" Jessica's jaw dropped. "You're kidding."

Ken shook his head. "I've never been more serious."

"Then you're just plain crazy. Start my own squad," Jessica repeated, laughing. "OK, imagine if you'd quit the football team and I told you, 'No prob, just start your own team!'"

"Why not?" Ken countered. "Give me one good reason it wouldn't work."

"OK, first of all, there's always been only one official cheerleading squad at Sweet Valley High. I mean, there are probably rules about that sort of thing."

"New clubs form all the time," argued Ken. "If you don't ask, how do you know they won't let you start up another squad?"

"Maybe," Jessica conceded. "But anyone who's any good is already on Heather's squad."

"Not true," said Ken. "There are tons of girls out there who'd like to cheer and would probably be good at it. Every time the squad has a vacancy, you get dozens of girls trying out for that one spot, right?"

"But what about uniforms? Where would we practice?"

"The cheerleaders have always had to buy their own uniforms," Ken pointed out. "As for practicing, come on. All those athletic fields? If you were willing to practice before instead of after school, you could take your pick."

"It could be done," Jessica finally had to admit. Despite herself, she was starting to get a little excited.

"You can do anything if you want it bad enough."

"My very own cheerleading squad." Jessica couldn't help it—a big grin spread across her face. "I won't have a cocaptain, not Heather or anyone else. I'll call all the shots—I'll be totally in charge!"

"Queen Jessica," Ken agreed.

"I'll write all new cheers—it won't be the same old stuff," she continued. "I'll do a talent search and hold my own tryouts. All new girls, a whole new attitude!"

Ken clapped. "That's the spirit!"

"Oh, Ken!" Jessica flung her arms around his

15

neck and gazed up at him with starry eyes. "You are just the sweetest, most adorable guy in the whole world, did you know that?"

"No, I didn't know that," he teased, wrapping his muscular arms around her slender waist. "Tell me again."

"You are just the sweetest, most . . ."

Ken silenced Jessica with a tender yet passionate kiss on the lips. *Everybody thinks my sister's such a brain,* Jessica thought as the kiss deepened and she abandoned herself to the delicious sensation. *But if you ask me, she's an idiot for letting Ken Matthews slip through her fingers!*

"You seem quiet," Todd observed to Elizabeth as he drove her home after the party. "Something on your mind?"

"Oh . . ." Elizabeth shrugged, looking away from him out the passenger-side window. "I guess I'm just still steaming about Heather. I kept telling Jessica to work with her, be flexible and open to new ideas and all that, but now I understand exactly how Heather made her feel and why she quit. That girl is a monster!"

"She's horrid," Todd agreed as he turned onto Calico Drive, "but Jessica will bounce back. She always does." The BMW rolled to a stop in front of her house. Killing the engine and the lights, he reached for Elizabeth. "Come here," he said softly.

Elizabeth let Todd pull her close and shut her eyes as he started pressing light kisses on her forehead, her temples, her cheekbones. But no matter how hard she tried, she couldn't give him her full attention. Her mind kept wandering, and it was leading her to the most disturbing places.

Jessica and Ken park like this now. Ken kisses Jessica like this. . . . Just thinking about it made Elizabeth's toes curl with envy. *I could be sitting in a white Toyota instead of a black BMW. I could be kissing Ken Matthews instead of Todd Wilkins.* . . .

Placing her hands on either side of Todd's face, Elizabeth gave him a kiss so boldly passionate, it made his eyes pop open in surprise. But it didn't work . . . not for her, anyway.

Elizabeth was still hiding it from Todd, but she couldn't hide it from herself. Lately Todd, the big love of her life, the boy for whom she'd given up all others, left her stone cold. She was starting to wonder: When she gave up Ken in order to save her relationship with Todd, did she choose the wrong boy?

Chapter 2

"Whoa, better call the *Sweet Valley News*," said eighteen-year-old Steven Wakefield with a teasing grin. "It's Sunday and she's out of bed before noon. I think this qualifies as a miracle!"

Jessica tightened the belt on her bathrobe as she entered the sunny Spanish-tiled kitchen. She stuck her tongue out at her handsome older brother, a prelaw student at the state university who often came home on weekends. "You've just forgotten what it's like to be young and fun and have a social life. Reading the business section of the newspaper—you look just like Dad!"

Over at the counter Mr. Wakefield was ladling batter into the waffle maker. "I get the feeling I was just insulted," he said, pretending to be hurt. "What's the matter with looking like ol' Dad?"

"Just kidding." Crossing the kitchen, Jessica stood on tiptoes to give her tall father a kiss on the cheek. "Steven's lucky he looks like you."

"If you think flattery will get you the first waffle, you're absolutely right," Mr. Wakefield said.

Jessica smiled. "You're easy, Dad."

She greeted her mother with a kiss, too. "I didn't expect you to be in such a good mood," Mrs. Wakefield admitted, giving her daughter an affectionate hug and then returning to the task of slicing a juicy cantaloupe. "You were pretty down in the dumps yesterday after the football game."

"Since then I've gotten a whole new perspective on the cheerleading situation," explained Jessica as she poured herself a cup of hot lemon-scented tea. "Ken had the absolute best idea."

"Let's hear it," said Steven, putting the business section aside in favor of the funnies.

"Well . . ." Jessica leaned back against the counter, facing her parents and brother. "I guess I don't have to remind you of all the underhanded things Heather Mallone has done since she moved to Sweet Valley."

"We've been hearing about it on a daily basis," Mr. Wakefield agreed, flipping the first crisp, golden waffle onto a serving plate.

"Because of her I quit the squad yesterday, and there's no way I'm going back as long as she's in charge."

"And it sounds like she's there to stay," observed Mrs. Wakefield. "So what did Ken propose?"

"I form my own squad," said Jessica, her eyes shining. "She stole the old one from me, but she

19

can't stop me from doing what I do best. I know I can get Maria and Sandy, and probably Lila, too, and then I'll audition a bunch of new girls. We'll show Heather what school spirit's really all about!"

"I think it's a marvelous idea," Mrs. Wakefield enthused. "Good for Ken. Good for you!"

"So you're going to start your own squad, from scratch." A mischievous smile creased Ned Wakefield's face. "Why, you should recruit your sister!"

At that moment Elizabeth appeared in the doorway. "Recruit me for what?" she mumbled sleepily, stretching her arms over her head and yawning.

Jessica tilted her head to one side, considering her father's suggestion. "You know, Dad," she mused, "you might be onto something. Think about the publicity we'd get with identical twins on the team!"

Steven snorted. Mrs. Wakefield smothered a smile.

"Recruit me for what?" Elizabeth repeated, still a little foggy.

Steven shook imaginary pom-poms. "Yay, team. Go, fight, win!" he cheered.

Elizabeth squinted at him suspiciously. Both her parents were now laughing openly. "Wait a minute. You're not talking about me cheerleading, are you?"

Her brother held up his hands, protesting his innocence. "Hey, I didn't start this."

Elizabeth whirled to face Jessica. "How many

times do I have to tell you I'd rather floss with barbed wire than be a cheerleader? Girls should play sports on their own, not just sit on the sidelines cheering on the guys!"

Jessica rolled her eyes; she'd heard this speech before.

"Besides," concluded Elizabeth, "you're not even on the squad anymore. How could you recruit anyone?"

"Never underestimate the powers of Jessica Wakefield," intoned Steven mysteriously.

Elizabeth looked to her parents for illumination. "Jessica's thinking of forming her own cheerleading squad," Mrs. Wakefield explained, "so she's in the market for athletic talent, and you naturally came to mind."

Elizabeth raised her eyebrows at Jessica. "Your own squad?"

Jessica smiled smugly. "Isn't it brilliant? Talk about the best revenge!" Her dimple deepened. "And it was all Ken's idea, can you believe it? I didn't think it could work, but he talked me into it. He really believes in me, and he wants more than anything to see me happy. Isn't that just so sweet?"

"Very," said Elizabeth, flouncing over to the counter to help herself to a waffle. "But just forget about trying to talk me into having anything to do with anybody's cheerleading squad under any circumstances."

Jessica feigned nonchalance. "Suit yourself," she drawled. "I just thought you'd be happy for me. I mean, about the cheerleading, and about Ken. My life is so fantastic! I'm going to be the captain of my own cheerleading squad, and I'm in love with the most wonderful guy. . . ." Jessica was pleased to note that Elizabeth looked a bit green. "It was just so romantic last night, Liz. He swept me off for this spontaneous late date. I mean, I couldn't stay in a bad mood. And today we're spending the entire day together at this little secluded beach he knows about. He says it's very private."

Steven made a gagging noise. "Do you mind? I'm trying to eat."

"Well, have fun." Sloshing some maple syrup onto her waffle, Elizabeth picked up her plate and headed for the door.

Before Jessica could tag after her sister and torture her some more with further details of Ken's devotion, the telephone rang. Mrs. Wakefield picked it up. "Hello? Hi, Amy. Yes, she's standing right here."

She held the receiver out to Jessica, who stuck her lower lip out in a pout. "If she's calling to beg me to rejoin the squad, she's wasting her breath," Jessica mumbled as she took the phone, although she hoped Amy was calling to do just that. "What's up?" she asked curtly.

"Did you hear the thrilling news?" said Amy, her voice pitched high with excitement.

"Don't tell me," guessed Jessica. "Heather was hit by a truck!"

"Now, don't be that way," said Amy in a manner that Jessica found annoyingly patronizing. "No, silly, we're going to regionals!"

Jessica gripped the edge of the counter for support. "You're kidding!"

"Nope, we're really and truly going," said Amy. "The American Cheerleading Association scout was at yesterday's game, and he told Heather he was extremely impressed with us, and that we're definitely regionals material. 'Regionals material'— those were his exact words. How exciting is that?"

Just a few weeks earlier Jessica would have been doing handsprings over news like this. But now, to think the squad was going to regionals without her . . . "I'm just busting," she said, gritting her teeth.

"You know . . ." Amy's voice became conciliatory. "You could still be on Heather's squad if you really want to, Jess. I'm sure she'd take you back if you apologized and—"

"Heather's squad!" Jessica exploded. "She would take me back if I apologized! I don't think so!"

"Well, fine," said Amy, becoming huffy. "If you're going to be that way about it . . ."

"You bet I'm going to be that way about it," declared Jessica, slamming down the phone without even bothering to say good-bye.

The call from Amy had taken away Jessica's appetite. Abandoning her lukewarm, syrup-soaked waffle, she trooped after her sister. It wasn't like Elizabeth to be antisocial, but she'd retreated to the den to eat a solitary brunch in front of the TV. Jessica peeked in at her. *I really got her goat when I started gushing about Ken,* Jessica thought, an amused smile curving her lips. She sprinted out of

23

the kitchen pretty darn fast—she just couldn't stand hearing about it!

Jessica reflected back on the dirt she'd discovered in Elizabeth's diary. She couldn't help being impressed that her boring, conservative, play-it-safe sister had played a role in such a melodramatic saga. First Todd had moved away—major heartbreak. Then Elizabeth had turned for comfort to Todd's best friend, Ken. Their friendship had blossomed unexpectedly into romance—major guilt. Unwilling to hurt Todd, Elizabeth and Ken had decided to do the right thing and forswear their secret love. Eventually, Todd had moved back to Sweet Valley, and he and Elizabeth had once again became a rock-solid steady couple. *But she never got over Ken,* Jessica surmised. *Not surprisingly, since he's a thousand times cuter and more fun than Todd!*

Jessica wondered what her sister's easygoing boyfriend would think if he found out that, unbeknownst to him, he'd been part of a love triangle involving his own best friend. Talk about fireworks!

She directed one last glance Elizabeth's way, then retreated back into the hallway. It gave her a feeling of power, having discovered this secret about her sister. *I know something about her that she doesn't know I know!* The question was how best to use this secret knowledge to her advantage. Because there was no doubt, at some time and in some way, she would use it. It was just too good an opportunity to waste!

❖   ❖   ❖

24

"I'm having a tough time concentrating on this history assignment," Enid admitted to Elizabeth on Sunday afternoon. "The sun just feels so good, I keep drifting off."

The two girls were reclining on lounge chairs by the swimming pool in Elizabeth's backyard, attempting to combine homework with sunbathing. As she pushed the loosened straps of her bikini top to the side in order to bare her smooth, golden-bronze shoulders, Elizabeth glanced at Enid. Her friend was lying flat on her back, her face tilted to the sky. "Maybe if you sat up in your chair and opened your eyes," Elizabeth teased. "I find it a lot easier to read that way myself."

Enid giggled. "What a novel idea. You think of everything, don't you?"

Enid adjusted the back of her chair to a vertical position and opened her history book with a sigh. A moment later she closed it again. "I still can't concentrate," she declared. "I think I'll cool off with a dip in the pool."

"I'll join you," offered Elizabeth, happy for an excuse to toss her own book aside. She was having trouble concentrating, too, but for a different reason. . . .

Enid swam a few laps of the pool at a gentle crawl with Elizabeth backstroking beside her. Then the two girls hung off the ledge in the deep end, their legs floating. "So where's Jessica today?" Enid asked idly.

"She went to the beach with Ken," Elizabeth answered, hoping she sounded casual and uninterested.

Because she felt anything but. She remembered Jessica's smug announcement that morning: "We're spending the whole day together at this little secluded beach Ken knows about. He says it's very private. . . ."

The worst thing was, Elizabeth knew exactly what beach Jessica was talking about. It had to be the same one she and Ken went to when they were seeing each other secretly!

Elizabeth felt as if she might go crazy if she pictured Ken and Jessica alone on the beach together one more time. But she couldn't stop thinking about it, and despite the agony it caused her, she found she wanted to talk about it, too. "What do you think about those two, anyway?" she asked Enid. "I mean, about them as a couple."

"Oh, I think they're perfect together," said Enid, to Elizabeth's dismay. "The star quarterback and the head cheerleader. . . or rather, the ex–head cheerleader." She ducked her head backward into the water to wet her hair. "They're both blond and gorgeous and outgoing and popular, and they really seem to be nuts about each other. This could be the guy Jessica gets serious about, don't you think?"

"I suppose." Elizabeth trailed her fingers in the water, then drew her hand back quickly when she realized she'd been sketching the initials "K.M." "Then again, in a day or two she could blow him off and get interested in someone new. You know how she is."

"Not everyone's cut out for monogamy," Enid

agreed. "But don't you think it's also partly a question of finding the right person? I mean, you and Todd have been together for a long time partly because that's your style, but mostly because you're totally right for each other. If Todd had turned out to be a different guy, you might be into dating around like Jessica."

Elizabeth pushed off from the side of the pool, rolling onto her back. Enid paddled after her. "You're probably right," Elizabeth said after splashing around for a moment. "I mean, don't get the wrong idea," she added. "I'm happy for Jessica, it's just that . . ."

What a liar! she thought to herself. *You're not happy for Jessica at all!* "What am I saying?" she burst out. "To tell you the truth, Enid, seeing Jessica and Ken together . . . it makes me feel . . . oh, I don't know."

Enid was always a good listener; now she waited patiently for Elizabeth to finish her thought. Elizabeth gazed at her friend's face, unsure. *I could just tell her everything, she considered. God, it would feel so good to get this off my chest! And Enid's always wonderful at helping me put things in perspective. . . .*

"You see . . ." Suddenly Elizabeth couldn't quite bring herself to do it. After so much time had passed, it would just be too hard to explain the whole complicated, sordid story. And what if Enid thought Elizabeth was horrible for going behind Todd's back like that, for lying to everyone, including Enid herself?

27

Late at night your emotions more easily get the upper hand, Elizabeth thought, remembering the tumult of feelings she'd experienced the previous night at the party, and then when she'd said good night to Todd, and then again when she was alone in her room. But in the bright light of day . . . The sun seemed to be trying to chase her secret feelings back into their hiding place. And maybe that's where they belonged.

"It's just a little weird, that's all," said Elizabeth. "I mean, Jessica's so moony about Ken because their relationship is new, and it sort of makes me feel like Todd and I are boring, you know?"

Enid nodded. "There's nothing quite like that brand-new-infatuation stuff," she said, "but you and Todd have something even better. Deeper, you know? It's real—it's stood the test of time."

"Yeah, you're right," agreed Elizabeth with false brightness. "You're absolutely right." Turning away from Enid, she swam to the ladder and climbed out of the pool. As she dried herself off, she made a decision. *I'll just have to keep it inside,* she told herself firmly, *and try harder to be happy with Todd, and happy for Jess and Ken.* Because Todd was her boyfriend, and Ken was her sister's boyfriend, and the sooner she got that straight in her mind, the better off she'd be.

Ken chased Jessica to the water's edge. She squealed with laughter as he picked her up easily and slung her over his shoulder fireman style, then waded with her into the surf. She beat playfully

28

against his back with her fists, but she wasn't trying too hard to get free.

A big wave rolled in, knocking Ken off balance. "Whoa!" he shouted. "Looks like we're going for a swim!"

They both got a thorough dunking. Jessica spluttered to the surface, laughing. Ken scooped her up in his arms, and she put her own arms around his neck. They bobbed in the water that way, gazing adoringly into each other's eyes.

"You look like a sea monster," she teased, plucking a piece of seaweed from his hair.

"And you look like a mermaid," he said, giving her a kiss.

His lips were wet and salty and delicious. "Umm," murmured Jessica. "Let's try that again. . . ."

A few minutes later, after toweling off and re-applying suntan lotion to each other's bodies, they were lying face-to-face in a pleasant tangle of limbs on the beach blanket. "How come when I see other couples acting all mushy like this, I think it's nauseating," said Jessica, nuzzling her nose against Ken's, "but when we do it, it's so much fun?"

He laughed. "Good question." He nibbled on her ear. "But it is fun, isn't it?"

Jessica sighed with pure happiness. "Um-hm."

"Anyway, that's why I brought you here, so we'd have privacy. I mean, just in case we couldn't keep our hands off each other or something. I mean, I sort of anticipated that that might be the case," he added with a sexy smile, "especially if you happened to be wearing a totally hot black string bikini."

29

"Sorry to be such a temptress," said Jessica.

Ken's grin widened. "Don't be sorry, I'm loving every minute of it."

Cuddling closer, Jessica rested her head on Ken's shoulder. For a moment they lay peacefully, listening to the lulling sound of the waves crashing on the shore. "I guess it really doesn't matter how we behave," she commented, "since there's no one here to see us, anyway."

"It's just you and me," Ken agreed. "We're the only two people in the entire world."

"Umm." Jessica rubbed her cheek against his neck. *That's the way it is when you're in love,* she thought. *Everything and everyone else seems to disappear. . . .*

Jessica's brain hadn't been completely erased, though. Suddenly the image of Ken and Elizabeth cuddling on a beach blanket popped, in an unwelcome fashion, into her mind. "So how many other girls have you brought to this secret beach?" she teased, hoping to coax a confession out of Ken.

"None. You're the first."

Jessica laughed. "Oh, c'mon. I bet you came here with Terri."

She could feel Ken shaking his head. "Nope."

"Not even with Terri?"

Ken and Terri Adams, the petite, pretty assistant manager of the Sweet Valley High football team, had been a steady couple for quite a while. They'd broken up not long before Ken had started showing an interest in Jessica. "Not even with Terri," Ken confirmed.

"There must have been someone." Propping herself up on one elbow, Jessica lightly traced a pattern on Ken's chest with her fingernail. "You can tell me. I won't get jealous."

Ken laughed. "Sorry to disappoint you, but I don't have that many skeletons in my closet. I guess I was saving myself for you."

Putting both arms around her, he pulled her close again. His mouth found hers, and he began kissing her hungrily . . . a kiss that left no room for doubt. She hadn't been able to trick him into saying anything about Elizabeth, but Jessica decided it really didn't matter. No matter what Elizabeth might be feeling, it was obvious Ken wasn't hung up on the past.

They stayed at the beach until the sun was low in the sky, a fiery red ball poised to drop into the western sea. "Are you hungry?" Ken asked as he pointed the Toyota back toward town. "I was just thinking I could go for a burger and shake."

"Sounds good to me. You can really work up an appetite lying on a beach blanket all day, huh?"

He flashed a smile at her. "All that heavy breathing burns a lot of calories."

Jessica rolled down her window, shaking her salty tangled hair in the wind. She couldn't seem to stop smiling. "This was a great day," she shouted to Ken over the pulse of the radio, "but for once in my life, I'm not sorry the weekend's almost over. Tomorrow at school I'm going to start recruiting my new cheerleading squad!"

Ken turned into the Dairi Burger parking lot. "I bet you won't have any trouble finding girls who want to cheer."

"But I'm only going to take the cream of the crop," said Jessica. "How do you think Elizabeth would be as a cheerleader?"

"Elizabeth?" Ken's eyebrows shot up. "As in, your sister?" Jessica nodded and Ken burst out laughing. "Elizabeth, a cheerleader," he repeated. "Sorry, I just can't picture it."

"I think she'd be great," argued Jessica.

"Yeah, but does she want to cheer?"

"It doesn't matter what she wants," said Jessica. "It's what I want!"

They were both laughing until, at the same instant, they spotted the white Mazda Miata convertible with the "CHRLDER" license plates. "Yuck," grumbled Jessica.

Ken put the key back in the ignition. "We could go someplace else," he offered.

"No," said Jessica. She wasn't about to let Heather Mallone scare her away from her long-time favorite hangout. "This is fine. Yesterday I thought I never wanted to lay eyes on Heather Mallone again, but now I actually wouldn't mind having a word with her."

There was no doubt that Heather had set out to take Sweet Valley by storm and that she was succeeding. As Ken and Jessica entered the Dairi Burger, their eyes were drawn immediately to a big table in the center of the restaurant crowded with laughing, chattering kids. Heather sat surrounded

32

by some of her new, admiring friends, a gang of very popular SVH seniors.

"Let's do take-out," Ken said in a low voice to Jessica. "Maybe you don't mind her, but she makes me sick."

They had to walk by Heather's table to reach the take-out counter. As they approached, the table fell silent.

Jessica felt all eyes on her, including Heather's. With her shoulders straight and her chin up, she met Heather's smirking, triumphant gaze head-on.

She thinks I'm just going to slink by all miserable and groveling, realized Jessica. *Boy, does she have me figured wrong!*

Instead of following Ken to the counter, Jessica pivoted on her heel and marched right up to Heather. "Congratulations, Heather," she said sweetly. "I hear you're taking your squad to regionals."

Heather blinked, surprised. Then she regained her composure. "That's right," she purred, obviously expecting Jessica to beg to be allowed back onto the squad.

"Well, good luck in the competition," said Jessica in the same bright, careless tone.

Tossing her hair, Jessica sauntered over to Ken. She knew Heather was staring after her. *Good luck is right,* she thought with a secret smile. *You're going to need it!*

Jessica knocked on Elizabeth's door when she got home. "Come in," Elizabeth called.

Elizabeth was sitting on her bed, a spiral notebook open on her lap. Jessica bounced onto the bed next to her. "Did you have a nice day?" she asked her sister.

Elizabeth shrugged. "Average." There was a pause. Jessica waited patiently. At last Elizabeth asked reluctantly, "How 'bout you?"

"Oh, it was divine." Jessica closed her eyes rapturously. "Ken is just . . ." She shook her head, dimpling coyly. "I don't think there are words to describe what it's like being with him. I mean, it's just . . . he's just . . . Oh, Liz, you can't even imagine."

Elizabeth tapped her pen on the notebook. "Do you mind?" she said sharply. "I'm kind of busy."

Jessica ignored this none-too-subtle hint. "I asked Ken about you," she told her sister.

Elizabeth's eyes bugged slightly; she looked as if she'd just swallowed something wriggly. "What . . . what about me?"

Jessica stifled a giggle. "I asked him if he thought you'd be a good cheerleader," she replied, all innocence.

Elizabeth sank back against the pillows. "Oh, cheerleading. Well . . . what did he say?"

Jessica didn't hesitate to put words in Ken's mouth. "Oh, he said you were probably too book-wormy to be a cheerleader."

"Oh, really." Elizabeth's tone grew huffy. "That's one way of putting it, I suppose. Another way of putting it is that I wouldn't be caught dead doing it."

"Really?" Jessica tilted her head to one side. "You mean, you've never wanted even a teeny,

34

weeny bit to be on the sidelines cheering for Todd on the basketball court, or say . . . Ken on the football field?"

Two spots of red stained Elizabeth's cheeks. "OK, Jess," she snapped, slamming her notebook shut. "I'm going to say this one more time and one time only, so listen good. I—will—not—under—any—circumstances—be—on—your—new—cheerleading—squad!"

"OK, OK." Laughing, Jessica put her hands up in an "I surrender" pose. "It's your choice, Liz, of course."

"You bet it's my choice," Elizabeth called after her as Jessica disappeared into the bathroom that connected their bedrooms.

In her own room Jessica went straight for the telephone. In quick succession she dialed three phone numbers: Lila's, Maria's, and Sandy's.

She had the same conversation with each girl. "Meet me tomorrow before homeroom," she instructed her friends. "I've got something extremely important and top secret to discuss with you!"

Next Jessica called Ken for a lovey-dovey goodnight chat. Then she showered, spent a few token minutes on homework, and got ready for bed.

Switching off the light on her nightstand, she cuddled under the covers, smiling happily to herself. She planned to have very satisfying dreams, about steaming up some car windows with Ken . . . and about knocking Heather Mallone and her lousy cheerleading squad right out of the regionals competition.

Chapter 3

Lila, Maria, and Sandy met Jessica by her locker Monday morning before school started. As soon as they were all there, Jessica whisked them into the girls' room for a private conference.

"So what's going on?" Lila demanded, whipping out a lipstick as she leaned close to the mirror to examine her flawless makeup.

"Yeah, what's the big secret?" asked Maria, fluffing her long brown hair with her fingers.

"I have a proposition for you," declared Jessica. Sandy was wearing a short denim skirt; Jessica eyed her calves critically, checking for muscle tone. "I hope you've been working out lately, Sandy, even though Heather kicked you off the squad."

Sandy wrinkled her nose, her hazel eyes puzzled. "Actually, I've kind of been blobbing out. I was just so sick of that totally obsessive diet-and-

36

fitness regimen Heather had us on, I figured I deserved a break."

Jessica turned to Maria. "I've been on a couple long bike rides, but that's about it," Maria said. "Why? What's this all about?"

"My new cheerleading squad, that's what this is all about!" said Jessica.

Lila froze with the lipstick an inch from her pursed lips. "Your new what?"

"Cheerleading squad," repeated Jessica, taking a small bottle of cologne from her purse and spritzing the base of her throat. "Ken helped me see that there was absolutely no reason I should let an upstart like Heather Mallone put an end to my cheering career. So I'm forming my own squad, and I'm counting on you three to be the foundation."

"Oh, Jessica!" squealed Sandy. She and Maria crowded close, bouncing up and down with excitement. "What a great idea!"

Lila finished painting her mouth, then tucked the lipstick back into her bag. "What's the point?" she drawled.

"What's the point?" said Jessica indignantly. "The point is this is my school and my sport, and if anyone deserves to go to regionals, it's me. And you two," she added, turning to Maria and Sandy. "Why should we be shut out from the glory we all worked hard for?"

"I'm with you one hundred percent," declared Maria.

"Me, too," said Sandy.

Jessica looked at Lila. "Sorry," said Lila. "There's a reason I quit the squad myself ages ago. Cheerleading is a bore, and the uniforms are tacky."

"It is not a bore!" Jessica protested. "And the uniforms don't have to be tacky. We're a new squad—we can buy the hottest, cutest uniforms out there."

"So, OK," Lila said, playing the devil's advocate. "So let's say the four of us have spiffy uniforms. We're still only four girls—hardly enough for a squad."

"I said you guys would be the foundation of the squad," Jessica pointed out. "You'll have to help me recruit the best dancers and gymnasts in the school. I know there's lots of talent out there just waiting to be tapped."

"Dancers and gymnasts?" Lila remained skeptical. "What do they know about cheerleading?"

"Nothing," Jessica said cheerfully. "But they'll have what it takes to turn into cheerleaders—strength, agility, grace, limberness, rhythm. We're just going to have to practice like mad and then get an audience with the ACA scout to get a slot in regionals." She shrugged. "Piece of cake!"

Lila had to laugh. "That's what I love about you, Wakefield. You're from another planet, but you act like you own this one. OK, sign me on."

"Hooray!" Maria gave Lila a hug. "We'll be cheering together again, Li. This is going to be so much fun!"

Jessica clapped her hands. "Enough of the love fest. We have business to attend to. First things first. Who should we recruit?"

All four agreed that two of their schoolmates were must-haves: Patty Gilbert and Jade Wu, two dancers who'd starred in the SVH variety show. "Patty especially would be great because she's so good at choreography," Jessica commented. "All right, we'll go after those two at lunch."

"If we can get them both, that'll bring us to six," said Maria. "Still a little skimpy."

"I'd prefer seven or eight," agreed Jessica.

"How about your sister?" suggested Sandy. "I always thought she'd be a terrific cheerleader."

"Funny you should say that," said Jessica. "Liz is on my list, too."

Lila laughed out loud. "You're kidding. Liz a cheerleader?"

Jessica brushed some blusher on her cheeks. "Why not?"

"You'll never get her on the team," Lila predicted.

"Wanna bet?"

"Sure, what'll it be?"

"Let's see. . . ." Jessica snapped the blusher compact shut. "How about since we were just talking about uniforms, whoever loses buys new uniforms for the entire squad?"

"Yow!" exclaimed Lila. "That would set you back big-time, Wakefield. You must be pretty sure of yourself."

Jessica smiled. "Oh, I am."

Lila narrowed her eyes suspiciously. "Hmm. Well, I still say your sister would rather be eaten alive by red ants than lift a pom-pom. You're on!"

Lila held out one perfectly manicured hand. Taking it, Jessica gave it a firm shake. Then she slung her arms around Maria and Sandy's shoulders and steered them back out into the hallway. "Are you ready?" she asked, her eyes sparkling. "Are you psyched?"

Maria and Sandy bobbed their heads. "You better believe it!" they chorused.

At lunchtime Jessica hunted down sophomore Jade Wu at a corner table with her boyfriend David Prentiss. "Jade, I need to talk to you about something," Jessica announced in an important and mysterious tone.

At the same time, Maria rounded up Patty Gilbert, who'd been sitting with her cousin Tracy, Tracy's boyfriend, Andy, DeeDee Gordon, and Bill Chase.

Jessica and Maria hustled the two girls outside to the courtyard. Patty's and Jade's jaws dropped when they heard Jessica's invitation. "Cheerleading?" said Patty, her big brown eyes widening. "Gee, Jess, it was sweet of you to think of me, but the cheerleading thing—no offense, but it never really appealed to me."

"I don't think I'd have the time," said Jade, ducking her head shyly. "What with dance class three afternoons a week . . ."

"Maybe you've never been into cheerleading, but this is going to be a whole new ball game," said Jessica earnestly, looking from Patty to Jade and back again. "I want my squad to be different, innovative. That's why I need your dance and choreography skills. This is our chance to experiment, to bring a whole new look and style to the art of cheerleading!"

Patty smiled thoughtfully. "When you put it that way, it sounds like a challenge. It sounds like fun."

Jessica and Maria both smiled encouragingly at Jade. "Dance class is pretty formal and structured," Jade reflected. "Maybe . . . maybe I'll give it a try."

Jessica gave her an impetuous hug. "That's all I'm asking," she said. "Just show up at our first practice at the far end of the football field tomorrow morning before school. And spread the word. I want you two especially, but everybody's welcome to show up at practice and try out!"

Back inside the cafeteria, Jessica and Maria joined Lila and Sandy. "My new squad is almost complete. Patty and Jade are onboard!" Jessica sang triumphantly.

"They've agreed to come to practice tomorrow morning, anyway," said Maria. "How'd you make out with Elizabeth?"

"About like we expected," Lila reported. "Let me see if I can remember her exact words: 'I'd rather walk down Main Street naked than put on a cheerleading uniform.'"

Jessica lifted her shoulders in a careless shrug. "Obviously you didn't take the right approach."

"Face it," said Lila smugly. "Your sister isn't going to join the cause. The rest of us will need uniforms, though. You'd better start looking for a part-time job to pay for them!"

41

Jessica just smiled. She had an idea about how to coerce Elizabeth onto the new cheerleading squad. *Lila just doesn't have the right leverage,* Jessica thought. *I'm going to ask Elizabeth in such a way that she just won't be able to say no!*

By the end of lunch period the rumor had spread like wildfire around the Sweet Valley High cafeteria. Dozens of girls of all shapes and sizes, freshmen through seniors, crowded around Jessica's table, pressing her for information.

"Is it true, Jessica? You're starting your own cheerleading squad?" sophomore Stacie Cabot asked excitedly.

"Can anyone come to the practices?" pert, slender Lisa Walton wanted to know.

"What if you don't have any experience?" asked Alicia Benson.

"When are tryouts?" Jennifer Morris wondered. "How many girls are you going to pick?"

Jessica fielded the questions with a feeling of pleased self-importance, basking in the glory of having all eyes in the room upon her.

All eyes . . . including those of Heather Mallone.

Heather was sitting with what was left of the old cheerleading squad. After glancing disdainfully at Jessica, Heather leaned over to whisper something in Amy's ear. Amy laughed hysterically.

The laughter didn't bother Jessica one bit. *If she's cracking jokes, then it proves she really feels threatened.*

And Heather had a very good reason to feel

threatened, Jessica decided as she surveyed the huge pool of potential talent surrounding her. All the eager faces and bodies made her realize that her dream really could come true. It wasn't just talk.

Jessica Wakefield's cheerleading squad was on its way!

Elizabeth was cooking dinner when Jessica breezed into the kitchen late that afternoon. "Yum, smells good," Jessica commented, leaning over the saucepan and taking a deep, appreciative sniff. "Chili and corn bread, my favorite."

"Wanna set the table?" asked Elizabeth.

"Sure." Opening a drawer, Jessica grabbed a handful of silverware, then turned back to her sister. "So it's pretty exciting, huh? Having everybody buzzing about my new cheerleading squad."

"It's the talk of the town," Elizabeth agreed, tasting the chili and then adding a few more shakes of cayenne.

"It looks like tons of people are planning to come to practice and tryouts," Jessica continued, "which is good, because then I can afford to be very selective."

"I'm sure some of the girls will turn out to be really good."

"So how about you?"

"How about me what?"

Jessica smiled. "You know. Have you given it some more thought? Will you come to cheerleading practice tomorrow morning?"

"I swear, Jess," exclaimed Elizabeth as she

stirred the chili. "You're completely dense, did you know that? How many times are you going to make me tell you that I have absolutely no desire—as in zero, zilch—to be a cheerleader?"

"Maybe I just haven't phrased the question in quite the right way," mused Jessica.

"It doesn't matter how you phrase it," Elizabeth declared. "The answer is always going to be no."

"No, no, let me try one more time," said Jessica. Putting down the silverware, she folded her arms across her chest and looked Elizabeth straight in the eye. Both her tone and expression grew more serious. "How about this: Please be on my cheerleading squad, Liz, or else . . . I'll tell Todd about your fling with Ken."

"You'll what?" Elizabeth dropped the ladle into the chili.

Jessica smiled. "You heard me."

A fiery flush swept across Elizabeth's face. She felt as if she'd just swallowed a chili pepper whole. "I heard you, but I can't believe . . . How did you— Ken didn't . . . ?"

Elizabeth bit off her question, realizing that she'd basically just acknowledged her guilt. Jessica was still smiling like a cat that held a mouse between its paws. "No, Ken didn't tell me," Jessica assured her sister. "A couple of days ago totally by accident I stumbled upon those photo-booth pictures of you and Ken hidden under your pillow."

"Oh, those." A wave of relief washed over Elizabeth. If that was all the evidence Jessica had against her . . . "Why, those don't mean anything.

We were just fooling around. Ken and I never—"

"And then I read your diary."

"You what?"

"I read your diary," Jessica repeated cheerfully. "I had no idea it was going to be so steamy, Liz! I mean, there I was back then stupidly trying to get you interested in meeting a new guy after Todd moved, and it turns out the whole time you were already cheating on him with Ken!"

"I wasn't—I didn't—" Elizabeth spluttered.

"Yes, you did." Jessica grinned. "You did, and then you came home and wrote about it. In great detail."

Elizabeth was speechless with fury. "I can't believe you read—and now you're going to—"

Jessica supplied the term cheerfully. "Blackmail you. So, what'll it be, Liz? Will you be on my squad, or should I call Todd right now?"

Elizabeth sucked in a hot, angry breath. "Jessica Wakefield, this is the meanest, nastiest, most underhanded thing you've ever done!"

Jessica shrugged off the criticism. "You should know," she said, her eyes sparkling wickedly. "I mean, when it comes to underhanded, you wrote the book . . . or should I say the diary? So." She posed the question one last time. "What'll it be?"

Elizabeth realized she didn't have a choice. Her sister had her between a rock and a hard place. The thought of putting on a cheerleading uniform and jumping around with Jessica and a bunch of other giddy females made her skin crawl. But the thought of Todd finding out about Ken . . .

"All right," Elizabeth choked out. "I'll be on your squad. But I'll get you back for this, Jessica. Mark my words!"

Smiling, Jessica reached for the phone. Elizabeth's hand shot out to stop her. "You said you wouldn't call Todd if I agreed!" she cried. "We just made a deal!"

Jessica laughed at Elizabeth's panic. "Chill out—I'm just calling Lila. She'll want to hear about this. I mean, not all of it," she teased, "just the part about your joining the team."

Jessica punched in Lila's number. "Hello, Li?" she said a moment later. "I'm at home with Liz, and she has something she wants to tell you."

Jessica held the receiver out to Elizabeth. "Go on, tell her," she hissed.

Elizabeth took the phone reluctantly. "Hi, Lila," she said stiffly. "Um, yeah, I do have some news. I've decided I'd like to try out for Jessica's new cheerleading squad." There was a pause; Jessica guessed that Lila was ranting on the other end. "What can I say?" Elizabeth finally concluded. "I changed my mind."

Jessica grabbed the phone from her sister. "What do you think of that, Li?" she asked sweetly.

"What are you doing to her?" Lila demanded. "Is she tied up? Are you torturing her?"

"I guess Liz has always had a secret dream to be a cheerleader." Jessica glanced at her sister, whose face was still red with fury. "So, Lila . . ." Reaching into her backpack, Jessica pulled out a copy of the latest Cheer Ahead catalog, which she

46

and Lila had been looking through during school that day. "I think the little red-and-white numbers on page fifty-four look pretty hot. You can order mine in size six!"

Turning her back on Jessica, Elizabeth stomped across the kitchen to stand at the stove, furiously stirring her pot of chili. Whistling cheerfully to herself, Jessica sauntered out into the hall.

She paused in front of the mirror hanging over the table in the entryway. She high-fived herself, smiling at her reflection. *Way to go, Wakefield!*

Chapter 4

Elizabeth was dreaming that Mr. Collins, her favorite English teacher and the adviser to *The Oracle,* had taken the computers and typewriters out of the newspaper office. "From now on we're not going to print the news," he announced, passing out pom-poms to the whole staff. "We're going to cheer it!"

In her dream Elizabeth stared in horrified disbelief at Mr. Collins. She could barely hear him because of the buzzing in her head. . . . What was that awful noise . . . ?

The covers went flying as Elizabeth sat bolt upright, her heart pounding. It was still dark out, but the clock radio on her nightstand was blaring loudly. She swatted the off button with a desperate, irritated gesture. "Six A.M.," she muttered, throwing back the covers and climbing out of bed. "I can't believe I'm doing this!"

48

Shuffling to her closet, she wrapped herself in her bathrobe. In the bathroom she splashed cold water onto her face. Now wide awake, she blinked at herself in the mirror. *I should have told Todd right off the bat about Ken. But now it's too late; he'd never understand why I waited this long, and my diabolical sister is going to use it to blackmail me for the rest of my life!*

At the bottom of the staircase Elizabeth glanced out the window in the front hall and shivered. The first light of dawn was just warming the eastern sky, but it looked damp and chilly outside. *As if cheerleading isn't an insult in and of itself,* she thought bitterly, *we have to practice in the middle of the night?*

She trudged into the kitchen, her slippers making protesting slapping sounds on the tile floor. Jessica, already dressed in hot-pink leggings and a bulky sweatshirt, stood at the counter measuring something into the blender. When Elizabeth appeared, Jessica tapped the lid onto the blender and hit the power button.

Elizabeth put her hands over her ears. "Do you have to do that?" she complained. "Some sensible people in this house may still be trying to sleep!"

Jessica flashed her sister a peppy, encouraging smile. "A good breakfast is very important," she declared. "Power drinks, my own special recipe. Low cal, high protein, and delicious." Stopping the blender, she dipped a finger in to sample her concoction. "Umm, taste." She poured a glass for

Elizabeth and then one for herself. "This certainly beats Heather's disgusting lettuce-and-wheat-germ diet!"

Elizabeth frowned at the thick beige liquid. "What's in it?"

"Yogurt, banana, strawberries, a splash of o.j., and this high-energy protein powder I bought at the health-food store. And try one of these." Jessica held out a basket with a cloth napkin over it. "Buttermilk bran muffins with apple and raisins. I made them last night."

Setting a good example, Jessica took a big swig of her power drink. Grudgingly, Elizabeth lifted the glass to her lips. "Do you like it?" Jessica asked hopefully.

The drink wasn't half-bad, but Elizabeth wasn't about to admit that. "Does it matter if I like it?"

"Oh, come on, Liz," Jessica said in a cajoling tone as she slipped an arm around her sister's waist and gave her a squeeze. "Now that we've come to this arrangement, why not make the best of it? It could really be a lot of fun. Look." Skipping across the kitchen, Jessica bent to pull something out of a large canvas sack. "Here are your practice pom-poms. Aren't they adorable? Aren't you getting psyched?"

Jessica pressed the red-and-white pom-poms into Elizabeth's hands. *My very own pom-poms,* Elizabeth thought, staring down distastefully at the emblems of her degradation. *I never thought the day would come . . . !*

Just touching them made Elizabeth's whole

body twitch. She tossed the pom-poms aside in disgust.

The gesture was lost on Jessica. "Oh, Liz." She clasped her hands together, her eyes starry. "Just seeing you with those pom-poms . . . You're going to make the most beautiful cheerleader! I can't tell you how often I've dreamed of this, of you and me, cheering together side by side. I'm so happy!"

Elizabeth was not happy, but Jessica didn't pause to give her a chance to express her feelings either way. "Cheerleading is a blast. It's my favorite thing in the whole world, and you're just going to love it. I promise!"

Elizabeth gave her sister a dirty look. Then she drained the rest of her power drink, placed the empty glass on the counter with a clunk, and marched out into the hall and up the stairs to take a shower and get dressed for practice.

Despite the early hour the Sweet Valley High football field was swarming with would-be cheerleaders. Jessica scanned the crowd excitedly. "Amanda Hayes and Sara Eastbourne," she said to Lila, pointing. "They're both fantastic dancers."

"They take class with Mr. Krezenski," remarked Lila, naming the world-famous dancer who had a studio in Sweet Valley. "Supposedly he's pretty tough."

"That means they're disciplined." Jessica nodded with approval. "They know how to work hard. I like that."

51

Elizabeth was sitting cross-legged on the ground a short distance from the other girls. "Liz looks totally unpsyched," observed Lila. "What kind of thumbscrews did you put on her to get her here?"

"She's here," Jessica said. "That's all that counts."

"It's great to see Lisa Walton," said Maria, "and Mandy and Patsy and Jennifer. And look! Danielle Alexander. Isn't she a ballet dancer?"

"This is sure going to be interesting," predicted Sandy.

Practice pom-poms in hand, Jessica waved her arms at the crowd of chattering girls. When they were all facing her and attentively silent, she flashed a big, welcoming smile. "Thanks for turning out!" she boomed in her best cheerleader's voice. "It's great to see so many people. Start stretching out, OK? And I'll tell you what I've got in mind for the week ahead."

Some of the girls wore sweatshirts over leotards and tights, while others were dressed in shorts and T-shirts. They all started stretching out their leg muscles, twisting at the waist, and loosening up their shoulders. Patty Gilbert, wearing flowered Capri tights and a matching cropped sport top, dropped to the ground in a perfect Chinese split. Jessica beamed.

"We'll meet out here every morning this week at the same time," she began, "and on Friday I'll hold official tryouts. I'm shooting for a squad of eight or ten girls—it all depends on how you do. So let's get fired up!"

Her words were greeted by an enthusiastic cheer. Jessica took a bow, then clapped for silence. "OK. Not including Lila, Maria, and Sandy, how many of you have cheerleading experience? Let's see some hands."

Not one hand was raised. "Hmm. Well, OK. How many of you have tried out for the squad before—the old squad?"

Three hands went up this time. Jessica nodded. "Right, I remember. How about the rest of you? Do we have any gymnasts out there?"

A number of hands went up in response to this question, and quite a few more when Jessica asked about dance—jazz, modern, and ballet. "You're all going to be super, I just know it," she concluded. "Now, what I'd like everyone to do is to spread out on the field in a line facing me. Sandy, Maria, Lila, and I are going to run through some basic moves for you, and then I want to see you give it a try."

Bending, she hit the play button on the portable tape player she'd brought with her. As the catchy beat of a popular song began pulsing out of the speakers, Jessica started moving her feet from side to side and clapping her hands rhythmically. Lila, Maria, and Sandy joined in.

"First, the feet," Jessica called out. "We can sway from side to side"—she demonstrated the motion—"or rock back and forth. We can lunge with one foot forward like this, and hop back. As for our hands"—she dropped her pom-poms—"we can make fists, blades, cups, and fans.

53

Different hand positions go with different arm movements. We use our arms dramatically—watch me sweep, thrust, punch, and slice—to create rhythm and balance, and to catch the crowd's attention."

Jessica had matched each term with a gesture, and she was pleased to see most of the girls successfully imitating her movements. She got them all sidestepping and snapping their fingers, then clapping. "As you know," she hollered, "cheerleading is about building excitement in the teams and the fans. You've gotta have the jumps, but you've also gotta have grace and style and a killer smile." She grinned widely. "And lung power. Let's hear it—let's hear you yell!"

She shouted a cheer and the girls on the field echoed her. "I can't hear you!" Jessica called teasingly, cupping a hand to her ear. "What did you say?"

"Go, fight, do it right, WIN!" the girls hollered.

All the girls were moving to the music, shaking their shoulders and clapping and smiling. Patty, Jade, Lisa Walton, Stacie Cabot, Mandy Farmer, Danielle Alexander, Jennifer Morris, Patsy Webber, Alicia Benson, Aline Montgomery, April Dawson, Leslie Decker, and, of course, Elizabeth. *What a great bunch!* Jessica thought. *I'm going to have the hottest cheerleading squad in the history of California. No, make that the history of the world!*

Fifteen minutes later she was tearing out her hair. "Great, you can do a perfect cartwheel, but

54

that's just not going to cut it," she said to Alicia. "We need to see you do a round-off, back hand-spring. Spot her, Lila, would you? And Jade!"

Jessica turned to Jade Wu. "Let's see you try that back crunch again."

Obediently, Jade bounced into the air, arching her back as if trying to touch her heels to the back of her head. Jessica shook her head. "Higher," she commanded. "Get some vertical. Jump!"

She whirled to face Danielle next. "Try that spread-eagle one more time."

Danielle flung her long blond hair back, her face determined, and then launched herself into the air. "No, no, no," Jessica moaned. "This isn't *Swan Lake*! Bounce off both feet—put some spring into it, and smile!"

Danielle grimaced. "I'm trying, but it doesn't come naturally," she grumbled. "Especially the smiling part!"

Jessica stepped back to get the big picture. Sara and Amanda both had great rhythm and lots of personality, but neither of them could jump more than a foot in the air if her life depended on it; gymnasts Lisa and Leslie could both do flips from a standing position, but when it came to stringing the jumps together with dance steps, they started tripping over their own feet; Danielle was clearly never going to be as comfortable in sneakers as she was in toe shoes; April, Jennifer, and Mandy were simply hopeless.

"Patsy Webber looks good," Lila said to Jessica,

"and she used to live in France. She'd really add some style, you know?"

Jessica watched as the tall, slender girl with the striking green eyes and short coppery-red hair attempted a split. Patsy got stuck halfway to the ground. "Are you kidding?" exploded Jessica, feeling as if she were about to burst a blood vessel. "She's about as limber as a plank of wood!"

"She needs some work," Lila conceded.

"All right. All right!" Jessica bellowed, turning off the music abruptly. The girls all froze. "All right," she repeated in a calmer tone, making herself smile. "Another thing that's crucial in cheering is coordination, and by that I mean doing your arm movements, footwork, and jumps in sync with the rest of the squad. It's all got to flow—you have to start thinking of yourselves as part of one body. If I'm sliding right, everyone's sliding right. If I go down in a split, everyone's going down, one after the other, without missing a beat. Right now I want you to pair up and work on performing side-by-side herkies."

The girls were all staring blankly at Jessica. "Go on and get started!" she commanded.

Still, no one budged. Then Patty cleared her throat. "Um, what's a herky?"

"What's a herky?" said Jessica in disbelief. "What's a herky?" Her voice rose to an indignant screech. "Are you trying to tell me that not one of you knows what a herky is, one of the most basic cheerleading jumps? Not one of you bothered to

56

study up a little before coming to practice? Not one of you—"

She was so frustrated, she couldn't even get the words out. "Well, you'll just have to . . . you'll just have to . . ." she sputtered. She hurled her pompoms onto the ground, preparing to stalk off the field. "Figure it out yourself!"

Elizabeth had been keeping a low profile, practicing the jumps by herself on the fringes of the crowd. Now, along with the others, she stared in shocked silence at Jessica's retreating back. *Wow, what a blowup. So much for Jessica's dream team!*

The girls began milling about, murmuring among themselves. Standing in a tight huddle, Lila, Maria, and Sandy appeared to be debating what to do next.

Patty Gilbert threw her hands in the air. "I don't know why Jessica bothered recruiting us for the new squad," she grumbled, "if she's not even willing to take the trouble to train us!"

As the girls began to disperse in confusion and disappointment, Elizabeth darted forward. "Wait!" she called. "Don't leave."

When the girls were gathered around her, Elizabeth gave them all a reassuring smile. "I know that sounded a little harsh," she said apologetically. "Jessica's pretty worked up about all this, and it looks like the excitement got the better of her. Having her own squad is a lot of responsibility—she's going to be learning some things from scratch just like you guys are. So don't give up, OK? Come back tomorrow, same time, same place."

Elizabeth's speech was received with nods and smiles. Relieved, she lifted a hand to wave good-bye as the girls headed across the field toward the school building.

I can't believe I did that. Elizabeth shook her head, disgusted by her own helpfulness. *I can't believe she threw a tantrum and I saved her skin.* Not that it wasn't typical! She bent to tie the lace of her sneaker, an ironic smile on her face. *Jessica bites off more than she can chew, and I end up covering for her. She really owes me. Boy, does she owe me!*

When Jessica turned to storm off the field, she was mortified to discover Ken standing just a few yards away. "Oh, God, I can't believe you saw that!" she exclaimed, flushing.

"Rough practice?" he inquired, slinging an arm around her shoulders.

"You could say that. How did I ever think this could work? Being a good gymnast or dancer simply does not automatically make you a good cheerleader. These girls are total novices. Not that the Sweet Valley squad was ever championship material, but at least everyone knew what a herky was!"

"They'll get it together," Ken predicted, massaging her shoulders with strong fingers. "It'll just take some time."

"Yeah, like a year," said Jessica. "The problem is, we only have a week or so if we want to get an audience with the ACA scout and qualify for regionals! Oh, it's impossible." She fought the urge to burst into tears. "You saw them, Ken. Even Maria and Sandy have lost their edge since Heather kicked them off the squad. What am I going to do?"

"I have one word for you." Ken held up his index finger. "Visualization."

Jessica blinked. "Run that by me again?"

"Visualization," Ken repeated. "It's my quarterbacking secret. If I want to complete a pass, I have to be able to see it in my mind's eye first, and feel my body executing it before I even move a muscle. And when I call plays? I've taught myself to use my brain in a certain way, to visualize where each player will be, how he'll move, how we'll all move together as one entity." He grinned wryly. "Sounds kooky, huh?"

"Visualization." Jessica was unconvinced. "Isn't that what just happened back on the field, when I looked at all those girls and realized they stunk?"

Ken laughed. "No, visualization isn't seeing what's there, it's seeing what you want to be there. It's focusing on images of perfection and internalizing them. I'm telling you, Jess, it's the only way you'll get your squad up to speed in such a short time."

"Visualization, huh?" Jessica's expression brightened hopefully. "You really think so?"

"You can get videos for pretty much every sport—I bet they have them for cheerleading, too."

"What do I have to lose? I'll try it," Jessica decided. She smiled, her eyes twinkling mischievously. "In fact, I'm trying it right now. I'm visualizing . . . you and me at Miller's Point."

Ken grinned as he pulled her close for a kiss. "Funny, I was visualizing the exact same thing!"

"You're pulling my leg," Todd said to Elizabeth that day during lunch. "You went to Jessica's cheerleading practice this morning?"

Enid was also gaping in astonishment at Elizabeth. "What possessed you?" she asked.

Elizabeth shrugged as she took her cheese, sprouts, and tomato sandwich out of her lunch bag. She didn't want this to turn into a big deal. "Does it really strike you as that bizarre?"

"Yes, because you've always hated cheerleading," said Enid, twisting the cap off a bottle of apple juice. "Just yesterday you totally bit Lila's head off when she asked you about trying out for the new team."

"I changed my mind," Elizabeth said somewhat defensively. "Jessica really needs my help, so . . ."

"Yeah, but we're talking about cheerleading, not homework or something." Todd laughed. "Is she paying you or what?"

Elizabeth cracked a weak smile, not wanting him to guess how close he was to the truth. "I'm sure she'll find a way to return the favor."

"I still can't picture it." Enid giggled into her straw, blowing bubbles in her soda. "Liz in a short skirt shaking some pom-poms!"

Todd grinned at Elizabeth. "I can picture it," he teased. "Yow."

"Well, I really admire you." Enid was clearly still trying to smother a smile. "I mean, this whole sisterhood thing, the way you and Jessica always come through for each other. It's pretty inspiring."

Inspiring, my—Elizabeth took a bite of her sandwich, even though she had absolutely no appetite. She couldn't admit it to Todd and Enid, but frankly, "the whole sisterhood thing" made her sick.

"So you're really going to try to do it," said a voice dripping with disdain.

Jessica was standing in the hot-lunch line with Ken. Now she turned, tray in hand.

As always, Heather looked perfect: her thick mane of icy-blond hair fell in glamorous waves, her makeup was understated but flawless, the bright turquoise scoop-necked dress clung to her curves, silver jewelry set off her suntan—even her sandals looked Italian, Jessica thought, and very expensive. Not to mention the pedicure! I hate her. I really hate her!

"Actually, I'm not going to try to do it," replied Jessica coolly. "I'm just plain going to do it."

"In your dreams." Heather's smug smile got under Jessica's skin like fingernails scratching a blackboard. "I heard your first practice was . . . rough, to put it politely."

Jessica's face flamed. "That's why it's called practice. When the time comes for the real thing—"

"And when will that be?" Heather countered. She laughed dismissively. "You'll never pull a squad together, Jessica, and even if you do, what's the point? You don't have a school to cheer for—I'm in charge of the one and only Sweet Valley High cheerleading squad. And nothing's going to change that!"

"I guess we'll see, won't we?" Jessica challenged. "We'll see who has the best squad— we'll see whose school this really is!" Tossing her hair, she turned a haughty profile to Heather. "Come on, Ken. We're holding up the line."

Out of the corner of her eye, Jessica saw Heather stalk away. "Good for you," Ken murmured in her ear. "Good for you, standing up for yourself and for your squad!"

Jessica forced herself to smile with confident nonchalance. Deep inside, though, she was shaking like a palm frond in the wind. She had laughed them off, but Heather's words had really hit home. "You'll never pull a squad together, and even if you do, what's the point? You don't have a school to cheer for. . . ."

For a second Jessica squeezed her eyes closed, remembering that morning's disastrous practice. I'm staking my reputation on my new squad, but what if we fall flat on our faces? It was too terrible to contemplate, but the possibility was there—she had to face it. Heather might be right; Jessica might be setting herself up for a humiliation even worse than that of being elbowed off the old squad.

Chapter 5

"Hi, guys," Jessica said to Amy, Annie Whitman, and Jean West on Tuesday as she put her lunch tray down on their table. "It looks like the coast is clear—no sign of Heather," she joked. "OK if I sit with you?"

The three girls exchanged uncomfortable glances. Jessica, busily peeling an orange, was oblivious. "I never see you guys anymore— Heather totally monopolizes you," she complained. "But I want you to know that I'm not holding a grudge—about this whole cheerleading thing, I mean. I'll still be your friend even though you're cheering with Heather instead of me!"

It was a pretty magnanimous statement, and Jessica expected Amy, Jean, and Annie to be grateful. Instead they looked as if someone had poisoned their lunches. "What's the matter, Amy?" asked Jessica. "Don't tell me you're bent because

I'm starting my own squad and didn't ask you to be on it. Of course if you want to try out, you're welcome—"

"It's not that," said Amy, tossing an anxious glance over her shoulder. "It's just . . ." Instead of completing her sentence, she started packing up what was left of her lunch.

"It's just what?" pressed Jessica.

Amy sighed. "Heather would get mad if she saw us . . . you know."

"No, I do not know," said Jessica.

Amy looked to Annie for help. "We don't want to jeopardize our positions on the squad," Annie explained. "So it's probably better if we . . ."

The three girls rose to their feet. Jessica stared at them. "You're kidding!" she exclaimed. "Are you saying you won't even have lunch with me because of what Heather might think?"

"It's nothing personal," Amy assured her.

"Baloney!" said Jessica. "C'mon, Jean. You have more sense than that. Are you afraid of Heather, too?"

"Sorry, Jessica." Jean lowered her eyelashes, embarrassed. "Better safe than sorry."

Amy, Jean, and Annie scurried off. *They couldn't get away from me fast enough—you'd think I was a leper or something!* thought Jessica indignantly.

She couldn't believe it—ditched by some of her closest friends! *Or at least they used to be my friends, until Heather stole them.* Suddenly Jessica felt like crying; she bit into a juicy orange section to hide the fact that her lower lip was trembling.

She was hurt by Amy, Annie, and Jean's rejection, but it also made her more determined than ever to throw herself heart and soul into her new cheerleading squad. *I'll show Heather,* thought Jessica. *I'll show them all!*

"There," said Elizabeth on Tuesday afternoon as she removed a sheet of paper from the printer in the *Oracle* office. As well as writing occasional feature stories, she had her own weekly byline called "Personal Profiles." "My column's finished. Do you want to look at it, Penny?"

"I'm sure it's fine." Penny Ayala, the newspaper's lanky, fair-haired editor in chief and one of Elizabeth's closest friends, quickly skimmed the piece. "And I'm glad you're done, because I have another assignment for you."

"What's that?" asked Elizabeth, curious.

"We need a story about Jessica's new squad battling Heather's for cheerleading supremacy at Sweet Valley High," said Penny, her hazel eyes twinkling, "and who better to write it than someone on the inside?"

Elizabeth turned away and started sticking notebooks and papers into her backpack. "I know I don't often turn down an assignment, but if it's OK, I'd rather not do this one," she told Penny.

"Why not?"

Sweeping a strand of silky blond hair back from her forehead, Elizabeth faced Penny again. "Oh . . . I don't know. Maybe I'm too . . . biased. Yeah, I don't think I could write an objective article about something I'm so intimately involved in."

"But it doesn't have to be objective." Penny laughed. "We're talking about cheerleading, not politics! Just make it entertaining. Talk to Jessica, talk to Heather. . . ."

"That's the thing." Elizabeth snapped her fingers, glad to have stumbled upon an airtight excuse. "Heather wouldn't grant me an interview in a million years. Jessica and I are public enemy number one as far as she's concerned."

"So forget the Heather-Jessica angle. Talk to the girls on the two squads. Get their perspectives."

Elizabeth slung her backpack over her shoulder. "OK," she agreed reluctantly. "I'll give it some thought."

She was on her way out the door when Penny called after her, "Hey, Liz, I even have a title for your story. 'The Pom-pom Wars.' Catchy, huh?"

The Pom-pom Wars," Elizabeth thought grimly as she walked down the hallway toward the main lobby. *Spare me, please!*

Halfway to the student parking lot, she remembered that she'd told Todd she'd stop by the gym when she was done at the newspaper office—he was playing in an intramural basketball tournament. She hesitated for a moment, about to turn back, and then continued on to the parking lot. *I just don't feel like cheering him on,* she decided. *I mean, I used to like it, when it was just for fun. But now that I'm trying to get into the cheerleading mentality . . .*

"Todd Wilkins, he's our man," Elizabeth muttered out loud. "If he can't do it, no one can!" *Ugh. What have I gotten myself into!*

As Elizabeth neared the Jeep, she noticed that a familiar white Toyota was parked just two spaces away. Not only that, but someone had just climbed into the Toyota's driver's seat and was belting himself in.

Ken rolled down the window and smiled at her. "Hey, how're you doing, Liz?"

She walked past the Jeep to stand somewhat awkwardly next to Ken's car. "Oh, I'm OK, I guess."

"I wanted to tell you, I think it's great that you've joined Jessica's cheerleading squad."

"Oh, yeah, well . . ." Elizabeth lifted her shoulders.

"I know it's not really your thing," said Ken. "Jessica thinks you're the best sister in the world for doing it."

Elizabeth gave him a brittle smile. "Does she? I don't suppose she told you that . . ."

She paused. Ken waited expectantly, a friendly, innocent light in his eyes. *He doesn't know,* Elizabeth realized. *He doesn't know Jessica found out about us, that she's blackmailing me.* ". . . that she had to twist my arm," she concluded somewhat lamely. .

Ken chuckled. "She's mastered the art of persuasion, that's for sure." He turned the key in the ignition, and the Toyota's engine rumbled to life. "See you around, Liz."

"So long."

Elizabeth settled herself into the Jeep, watching Ken's car in the rearview mirror until it disappeared. She realized her pulse was racing, and when she checked her reflection in the mirror, her cheeks were pink and her eyes bright. *How can Ken have that effect on me?* she wondered irritably as she backed out of the parking space. It wasn't even a good conversation!

But he did have that effect on her . . . no doubt about it.

The black BMW rumbled to a stop just a few feet short of the guardrail at Miller's Point, a dead-end road in the hills above Sweet Valley. Todd let the engine die, then switched off the headlights.

For a few minutes he and Elizabeth sat in comfortable silence, gazing out at the velvety-blue night sky, the lights of the town twinkling in the valley, and in the distance the Pacific glinting silver in the moonlight.

Todd slipped an arm behind Elizabeth's shoulders. Automatically, she shifted in her seat, turning to face him. Gently, he placed a hand on each side of her face. She closed her eyes as he began to kiss her.

"Liz."

Elizabeth blinked. "Liz," Todd repeated.

"Hmm. What's the matter?"

He pulled back from her slightly and peered into her face, a puzzled frown creasing his forehead. "Nothing's the matter . . . with me." He dropped his eyes. "But I can tell you're not into it."

69

Elizabeth bit her lip. There was no point pretending her reponse to Todd's kisses hadn't been lukewarm at best. "I'm just . . . I don't know," she mumbled.

"Is something wrong?" Todd asked, a note of fear entering his voice. "Is it me?"

"Oh, no, of course not," Elizabeth hurried to assure him, even though there was something wrong, and it *was* him, in part.

"Because I've been getting the feeling lately," continued Todd, looking straight ahead through the windshield, "that you're . . . bored or something. With me. With our relationship."

"That's simply not true," declared Elizabeth, tugging on his arm until he turned toward her again. "I've been kind of busy and preoccupied, that's all. And tonight . . ." She stifled a yawn. "I'm just plain exhausted. I was up before dawn for cheerleading practice," she reminded him with a wry smile.

Todd gazed down at her, studying her face. She tried her best to look loving and sincere.

At last the worried expression left his eyes. He folded her in a tight hug. "Sorry to be so paranoid," he whispered into her hair. "I'm just so crazy about you. I don't know what I'd do if you stopped loving me."

Todd's mouth found hers and once again they were kissing. This time Elizabeth made an effort to be more responsive. It wasn't that hard. As she tangled her fingers in Todd's hair, she imagined it was blond instead of brown; she pretended she was running her hands over another boy's shoulders, rubbing another boy's broad, hard, sexy back. . . .

When Todd started up the car a while later and did a U-turn to head home, Elizabeth found herself feeling incredibly guilty. Not only had she lied to Todd again, saying there was nothing wrong, but she'd convinced him that nothing was wrong by pretending she was with another guy! It was almost as bad as actually cheating!

And the worst part was Todd still didn't suspect a thing. He was humming to the song on the radio, the corner of his mouth curved slightly upward in a soft smile.

As they bumped back onto the main road, the headlights of another car crossed theirs. The car was turning off at Miller's Point; curious, Elizabeth glanced over to see if it was anyone she knew.

There were two people in the white Toyota—two blond heads, his and hers, one with short hair, one with long. Ken and Jessica, in quest of a romantic interlude. *Why does it bother me so much, and when is it going to stop bothering me?* Elizabeth wondered, a sick, sharp pain in her chest. *When am I going to forget about Ken?*

As soon as Ken dropped her off, Jessica pounded up the stairs and rapped on her sister's door. "Can I come in?"

"I'm about to go to sleep," Elizabeth replied, her tone discouraging.

Jessica pushed open the door and charged in

71

anyway. "But you're not asleep yet!" she observed cheerfully.

Elizabeth was reading in bed. She scowled at her sister. "I'd like to be."

"Well, I personally am never going to be able to fall asleep," Jessica declared, ignoring her sister's broad hint to get lost. "I'm just tingling from head to toe, you know? My whole body is like . . ." She dropped onto Elizabeth's bed, bouncing. "I was with Ken," she explained, a sly smile in her eyes. "He just gets me so . . ." She nudged Elizabeth's knee under the covers. "Well, you remember."

"I'm afraid not," Elizabeth said coldly, looking back down at her book.

"Oh, come on, Liz," Jessica teased. "I read your diary, or did you forget?" She didn't like thinking about Ken kissing her sister, but it definitely made her feel a lot better to remind Elizabeth repeatedly that these days Ken was kissing her. "Isn't he a great kisser? He has the best lips. Not too hard and not too soft. I hate guys with squishy lips, don't you? But Ken's are perfect. Umm—just thinking about it!"

Elizabeth slammed her book shut. "OK, I'm ready to turn my light out. Do you mind?"

Jessica grinned impishly. "No, I'm not leaving until you admit that Ken Matthews is the best kisser of any boy you ever went out with, including Todd."

"I can't believe how infantile you are!" cried Elizabeth. "Will you just get out of my face?"

"Admit it," Jessica pressed. "Ken's the best kisser."

Elizabeth shook her head stubbornly. "To tell you the truth, I hardly remember," she said, reaching for the light switch. "Good night, Jessica."

The room was plunged into darkness. "Night, Liz," said Jessica, rising. "Oh, I almost forgot—I'm holding an extra practice tomorrow afternoon, here at our house. I ordered a visualization video from Cheer Ahead, and they're sending it overnight mail—we're all going to watch it together. And don't think you don't have anything to learn from this, Liz, just because your jumps are already pretty good. I want to see you put your whole heart and soul into this. You're a cheerleader now—be proud!"

Her face buried in her pillow, Elizabeth grumbled something inaudible. Something profane, probably, Jessica thought with a grin. "Sleep tight, Liz," she said. "And try to dream about cheerleading, OK?"

There was a muffled click as Jessica shut the door to the bathroom behind her. Elizabeth kicked the covers off, then pulled them back again; she tossed from one side to the other, trying to get comfortable. But her eyes were wide open in the dark, and suddenly she wasn't the least bit tired.

Jessica had gone to her own room, but her words seemed to linger in Elizabeth's. "I'm tingling from head to toe. . . . Admit it, Ken's the best kisser. . . ."

Elizabeth had said she didn't remember. But that was yet another lie. She put her hands to her cheeks, feeling how red and hot her face was. The trouble was she did remember what it was like to kiss Ken—all too well.

Reaching up, Elizabeth turned the lamp on her nightstand back on. She swung her legs over the side of the bed and crossed to her desk. She'd hidden her diaries in the bottom drawer, under a pile of old school notebooks. *Not that that stopped Jessica!* she thought bitterly.

She took one of the volumes of the diary back to bed. Propping up her pillows, she sat up with the covers pulled over her lap and let the diary fall open in her hands. As if the emotions recorded there were especially strong and vibrant, it opened automatically to a page on which she'd written about Ken.

Elizabeth read the entry: "I can't believe I let myself get so carried away. . . . Diary, I've never felt so bad—and so good—at the same time. Ken kissed me like no one's ever kissed me before. . . ."

She'd written Ken's name over and over in the margins, the pen biting deep into the paper. The journal was so intense, so personal. *And Jessica read it—she read it all!* Elizabeth thought, feeling angry and violated. "I shouldn't have written about it," she murmured out loud to herself. "I should have kept it to myself, locked in my heart. It was our secret, Ken's and mine."

With a sigh Elizabeth returned the diary to the desk drawer. Lying in the dark again, she wrapped her arms tightly around a pillow. Right before she drifted off to sleep, the thought flashed across her

74

mind: *Oh, Ken, if I could only hold you in my arms one more time. . . .*

The dream was bizarre and yet vivid. Elizabeth sat on a throne on a stage. First Heather Mallone and the SVH cheerleaders revved up the audience as the marching band performed a lively tune. Then Todd and Ken appeared, both dressed in their sports uniforms. One at a time they walked across the stage toward her, bowed to her, and then bent to kiss her, once, twice, three times. Elizabeth considered each kiss carefully, and then the scores flashed onto the scoreboard. Ken received two 5.9's and a perfect 6; the cheerleaders hopped about, cymbals clashed, the audience cheered lustily. But Todd—Todd's performance disappointed everyone, including Elizabeth. She wanted to be generous, but she simply couldn't score him higher than two 4's and a 3.8.

Her lips still burning from Ken's dream kisses, Elizabeth opened her eyes to the gray light of dawn spilling into her shadowy bedroom. *This is terrible,* she thought, reflecting on the dream, and then remembering her date with Todd the night before. *I'm obsessing about Ken even more than I did back when we were involved with each other!*

It had to stop—that much was clear. But how? How to get over Ken the second time around?

That's the whole problem, Elizabeth realized. *I can't expect to get over Ken a second time when maybe I never entirely got over him the first time.*

She recalled the conversation she'd had a few days earlier with Mr. Collins. She'd asked for advice on behalf of a romantically confused "friend," and Mr. Collins had said, "It sounds like whoever she is still has some unresolved feelings for this other guy. She should try to work those feelings out before they destroy her relationship with her boyfriend."

Mr. Collins was right—he's always right, Elizabeth recognized. Harboring these secret feelings wasn't fair to Todd, or to herself. But how on earth was she supposed to "resolve" them? How could she find out how she really felt about Ken Matthews when he was happily dating her own twin sister?

Chapter 6

"No offense, but I don't think this is going to work," Patty said to Jessica on Wednesday after school. "How can just watching a tape on TV improve our skills?"

"I agree," said Elizabeth. "Wouldn't the time be better spent practicing?"

At Jessica's request, all the girls interested in trying out for her cheerleading squad had gathered at the Wakefields' house after school. Jessica herded them into the den. "The woman I talked to on the phone yesterday promised me this would make a huge difference," she said, doing her best to hide her own skepticism. "All kinds of athletes use these visualization tapes—tennis players, golfers, football quarterbacks . . ." She winked at Elizabeth. "Let's just give it a try, OK?"

Lila continued to grumble as the girls sat down in a circle facing the TV. "It sounds like New Age hocus-pocus to me."

"Tell me about it," Jessica hissed in Lila's ear as she tore the shrink-wrap off the video. "But I'm desperate!"

She stuck the tape in the VCR. Immediately a peppy musical theme blared over the speakers. Then two girls in tight, short orange-and-black cheerleading uniforms bounced into view. "Hi!" one of the girls chirped. "I'm Rosita and this is Amber, and we're cocaptains of the Fort Bridger, Texas, cheer squad, last year's national high-school champions!"

"And we're here to show you some of our best stuff," Amber piped in, "so your squad can start capitalizing on its own best qualities and talents to become the best you can possibly be!"

This perky announcement was met with groans from the Sweet Valley girls. "I think I'm going to be sick," mumbled Elizabeth.

"I bet they came in first because their uniforms are so skimpy," speculated Maria.

Jessica felt like gagging, too, but she wasn't about to let her squad quit before they even really got started. She whistled for silence. "C'mon, keep quiet! They take cheerleading seriously in Texas—I bet we can learn a lot from these girls."

The visualization video lasted twenty minutes. Amber, Rosita, and their teammates ran through a series of jumps, dance steps, and combinations, filmed from a variety of angles and sometimes in slow motion. There was very little narration; instead a musical sound track set the mood. In spite of herself Jessica found herself tapping her foot and snapping her fingers. Every now and then one of her muscles twitched; she realized she was literally itching to get out there and try some of the jumps. *Look at the height she's getting on that stag leap!* Jessica marveled silently, staring enraptured at the screen. *I never thought to try that arm position—doesn't that look sharp!*

When the tape ended, Jessica hit the rewind button and they watched it again. After the second time she rewound the tape and turned off the TV The girls rose to their feet, stretching. "So what did you think?" Jessica asked eagerly. "Wasn't that cool? I saw a bunch of stuff the second time through that I didn't even notice the first time—I started focusing on their footwork, you know?"

Lila, Jade, and Patty nodded; a couple other girls shrugged. The rest were looking at their watches and edging toward the door. "Well . . ." Jessica said, thinking maybe she should be satisfied with the fact that they weren't griping and complaining anymore, "let's think about what we saw, OK? Let it sink into your brain. Tomorrow we'll practice twice, before and after school. And then I guess we'll see if this visualization stuff is all it's cracked up to be!"

"Thanks for letting me interview you, Heather," Elizabeth said. "This will definitely make my story more rounded."

She'd cornered Heather in the lunch line, and after a momentary show of reluctance, Heather had agreed to step out to the courtyard for five minutes or so. They sat side by side on a bench; Elizabeth's pen was poised over her notebook.

"So you're writing an article about Jessica's new cheerleading squad," Heather said with a sniff.

"It's called 'The Pom-pom Wars,'" Elizabeth told her.

Heather laughed heartily. "That's hilarious. Really, Liz, you have a great sense of humor, using the word 'war' when you know it's going to be more like an overthrow."

"So you don't think Jessica will succeed at forming her own cheerleading team?"

Heather shrugged. "Maybe she'll form a team, but I honestly don't expect any competition from them—or should I say you? Anybody can mail-order cheerleading uniforms, but looking cute is no substitute for talent."

Elizabeth bristled at this thinly veiled insult. "Back to Jessica's motivation," she said, a bit more aggressively. "You antagonized Jessica until she felt she had no other option but to quit the squad, right?"

"That's one version of the story," said Heather.

"And before that, you got rid of Sandy and Maria," Elizabeth pressed. "That leaves you with a squad of just four. Do you really think four girls can represent the entire Sweet Valley High student body? Do you really think being cutthroat and elitist is a good way to exhibit school spirit?"

"It's not the purpose of the cheerleaders to 'represent' the student body,'" said Heather coldly. "Our job is to be the very best—that's how you build pride in your school, not by encouraging me-diocrity."

Elizabeth scrawled a few last words and then slammed her notebook shut. She didn't think she could keep a lid on her temper if she had to spend another minute with Heather Mallone. "Thanks for your time, Heather," she said, rising.

"No problem." Heather also got to her feet. Flinging her long blond hair over her shoulder, she tapped Elizabeth's notebook with a sharp cherry-red fingernail. "And I'm glad to see you haven't quit the newspaper because of cheerleading. You wouldn't want to put all your eggs in Jessica's flimsy basket!"

Pivoting on one high heel, Heather breezed back into the cafeteria. Elizabeth followed, her eyes blazing with suppressed fury.

She found Jessica sitting alone at a corner table. "Let me guess," Jessica said when she saw her sister's face. "You just had a conversation with Heather Mallone."

"She's the worst!" Elizabeth exclaimed.

Jessica rolled her eyes. "Tell me about it."

Elizabeth sat down. "I mean, of all the unpleas-ant, self-centered, ice-cold—"

Jessica laughed. "I hope that's the way you're going to describe her in your newspaper article!"

"I'm tempted to, let me tell you," said Eliza-beth.

Jessica had been writing something on a piece of notebook paper. "What's that?" Elizabeth asked.

"I'm trying to write a new cheer," said Jessica,

turning the paper so Elizabeth could see her scribbles. "But I'm not feeling terribly inspired. Every time I picture those girls jumping . . ." She grimaced.

"So you do the best with what you've got," said Elizabeth. "You look for ways to make them look better than they are."

Jessica snorted. "I'm a cheerleader, not a magician! And right now I feel dumb, dumb, dumb. I've been sitting here for fifteen minutes, and I can't think of any words to rhyme with 'beat.'"

"Heat," suggested Elizabeth. "Meet, greet, feet, neat, cheat, seat, treat—"

"Whoa, hold on!" exclaimed Jessica, laughing. "Let me write these down." She jotted down the words and then looked up at her sister with a grateful smile. "Thanks a lot, Liz. You're a lifesaver."

"I'd be happy to help you write the cheer," Elizabeth offered, "if you explain the code you're using."

"Really?" Jessica looked surprised and pleased. "You'd do that? I mean, even though I—um—coerced you into doing this?"

"Talking to Heather led me to the conclusion that your new squad is the best thing that could have happened to cheerleading at Sweet Valley High," declared Elizabeth. She smiled wryly. "Of course, the second-best thing would've been if you'd left me out of it!"

"You know," Lila said to Jessica on Thursday afternoon, "I hate to say it, but I think they're looking better. I think that dumb visualization tape actually helped!"

Pom-poms on their hips, Lila and Jessica stood at the edge of the athletic field watching the other girls practice. Jade sprang onto Patty's shoulders, then jumped off, executing a perfect side banana before landing lightly on her feet. Meanwhile, Sara and Amanda were spotting each other for round-off, back-handspring runs. Lisa, Stacie, and Jennifer were attempting jumps they'd been afraid to try the day before. Even Elizabeth, Maria, and Sandy, whose jumps were already technically strong, seemed to be performing their moves with added zest and style.

"Putting it all together will be the hard part." Jessica felt her spirits lift. "But I *am* starting to think there's some hope!"

"Having her at the other end of the field really cramps my style, though," commented Lila. "Doesn't it make you self-conscious?"

Jessica's gaze shifted along with Lila's. A hundred yards away Heather was practicing with her squad. At the moment she had stopped to watch Jessica's group, her arms folded across her chest and a disdainful smile on her lips.

Heather said something to Amy, who laughed loudly. Then they turned away and to rejoin their squad. Heather clapped her hands and shouted; the girls fell into line and like clockwork, chanting loudly, pranced their way through a lively, complicated cheer. Every jump and step was elegant, athletic, precise; the whole look was polished and tight. As much as she would have liked to find fault, Jessica couldn't spot a single error. *Championship material,* she thought gloomily. *They're as good as Rosita and Amber and the Fort Bridger girls!*

"Thank God she didn't see us practicing before the visualization video, huh?" said Lila.

"We're making progress, but there are a lot of rough edges," Jessica agreed dismally. "We have a long way to go. A long way."

"Liz, could you help me for a minute?" Jade called.

Elizabeth dropped her pom-poms and hurried to Jade's side. "What's up?"

"I'm working on my trojan," Jade explained, "and I think I have the leg positions down. One leg is tucked up and bent at the knee while the other is extended straight back, toe pointed. But I can't remember where my arms are supposed to be."

As Elizabeth demonstrated the jump for Jade, she realized someone was watching them. When she turned to see who it was, her heart did a round-off, back handspring.

Ken, wearing sweatpants and a cutoff T-shirt over his football shoulder pads, stood at the edge of the field, his helmet cradled under one arm. He lifted a hand in a wave; Elizabeth waved back.

Then she saw him smile; he put a hand to his mouth and shouted something. "Looking good, Jess!"

Jess. Elizabeth turned back to Jade, swallowing her disappointment. *Of course he wasn't looking at you*, she chastised herself. He was waving and smiling at Jessica—Jessica was his girlfriend, not Elizabeth.

As she left Jade practicing on her own, Elizabeth repeated the silent lecture. *He's not here to watch me, he's not here to watch me. He doesn't think about me anymore—as far as he's concerned, we're ancient history.*

It didn't help a whole lot. Elizabeth still felt the adrenaline surging through her veins; she was buoyed up on a wave of energy and excitement, just because she knew Ken was near. Taking a deep breath, she launched into a tumbling run: round-off, back handspring, back handspring.

After landing the second back handspring, she shot straight into the air in a perfect split jump. Then she dropped to earth, squatting on one knee with her breath coming fast, pom-poms at her waist.

She heard someone clapping and cheering. "Liz, that was fantastic!"

It was Jessica. Hopping up, Elizabeth glanced over at her sister as she shook out the muscles in her legs.

Ken stood at Jessica's side, an arm around her waist. They both gave Elizabeth a thumbs-up sign. Elizabeth smiled, feeling light-headed from her exertion and from the knowledge that, no matter how casually and how briefly, Ken's eyes had rested on her. The chant in her brain changed. *He was watching me, he was watching me . . .*

❀   ❀   ❀

On Friday afternoon Jessica pressed the play button on her portable tape player and then dashed over to line up with her cheerleading squad. She'd made final cuts and only the cream of the crop remained: herself and Elizabeth, Lila, Maria, Sandy, Jade, Patty, and Sara. And in their beautiful new red-and-white uniforms, compliments of Lila, they looked sharp and professional. As the fast-paced music started—Patty and Jade had picked out the songs—the line shimmied sideways, arms flying and pom-poms shaking. "We're turning on the heat!" Jessica and the other girls yelled. "We're the team to beat!"

In quick succession each girl in line stepped forward and performed a jump. Lila did a fabulous side-kick, Y-leap combination; Patty did a double herky no problem; Elizabeth's trojan-crunch combination was textbook perfect; and Jade, the last to go, amazed them all by landing her jump in a split.

Jessica couldn't contain her enthusiasm. She threw her pom-poms in the air, shouting joyfully, "That's it, you guys. You've got it!"

With double practices every day, and the constant reminder of Heather's squad's perfection at the other end of the field—the standard to meet and beat—it had been an emotional, exhausting week. Now the girls jumped up and down, hugging each other. Retrieving her pom-poms, Jessica waved them triumphantly. "Let's hear it. Give me a V!" she cried, grinning broadly. "For visualization!"

*　　*　　*

"Congratulations. I knew you could do it!" Ken exclaimed, striding toward her. "You really whipped the squad into shape. You guys look awesome!"

Elizabeth was standing slightly apart from Jessica and the other girls. She froze, her eyes widening. "Ken, it's—"

"A miracle," he said, wrapping his arms around her. His T-shirt was damp with sweat; he smelled like fresh-cut grass and some musky deodorant. A shiver ran down Elizabeth's spine. "I'm so proud of you, Jess, I could just . . ."

Ken drew her nearer, lowering his face to hers. He was about to kiss her . . .

Elizabeth stiffened and Ken stopped, his lips just inches from hers. For a split second they stared into each other's eyes, startled, and then they quickly stepped away from one another, laughing awkwardly. "Sorry about that," Ken murmured, his face reddening. "I didn't mean . . . I thought you were . . ."

"Easy mistake to make," Elizabeth assured him, her own cheeks flaming. "Don't worry about it— happens all the time."

Patting her on the arm, Ken hurried off to find the girl he'd meant to kiss. Elizabeth stood looking after him, still blushing. She realized her whole body was trembling. Ken always did have that effect on her. . . .

A short distance away Ken grabbed Jessica by the waist and lifted her high into the air, then lowered her to the ground again so he could plant a big kiss on her lips. Elizabeth turned away from the sight. She wanted to forget that Ken belonged to Jessica now—she wanted to treasure the feeling he'd left her with.

Because she couldn't deny it. She loved Todd, and she wanted to be loyal to him, but at that moment he was the furthest thing from her mind. Elizabeth hugged herself, savoring the memory. She couldn't deny how wonderful it had felt to be in Ken's arms again, even by accident, even just for a moment.

"You'd better not make that mistake too often," Jessica teased. "I know we look a lot alike, but by now you're supposed to know who's who!"

"It's the cheerleading uniforms," Ken protested. "And from a distance, from the side . . ."

Ken reached out to hug her again, tickling her. Jessica laughed. *How silly!* she thought to herself. A second before, when she'd seen Ken hug Elizabeth, she'd actually felt a flash of jealousy. They looked so good together, and she couldn't help wondering, Did they feel good together? Jessica was pretty sure Elizabeth still pined for Ken; did Ken still carry a secret torch for Elizabeth?

Of course he doesn't, she told herself as Ken's lips met hers in a sweet, searching kiss. She could feel him focusing on her, head to toe, his whole body and soul. They were so full of love for each other, sometimes Jessica thought they would spontaneously combust. No, there wasn't any room in

Ken's heart for those old forbidden feelings for Elizabeth.

Jessica gave Ken a last peck on the cheek. "We're going to run through the new routine one more time. Watch us, OK?"

"You bet," he said with a loving smile.

Jessica fairly floated across the grass. *This is what it's all about,* she thought happily as she turned up the volume on the tape player so that the music was really blasting.

She had her identity back. She was Jessica Wakefield, captain of the hottest cheerleading squad in Sweet Valley. And while she was ready to cheer her heart out for all the Sweet Valley High athletes, she knew she would shine brightest when the football team was on the field . . . and she was cheering for Ken.

"I can't believe it," Amy gasped. "Those can't be the same girls we saw practicing earlier in the week!"

Heather's eyes were also fixed on the rival squad. As Jessica and her team shimmied and shouted their way through a flashy routine, Heather nearly swallowed her gum. "They're good," she admitted grudgingly. "They're very good."

Annie had come to stand next to them. "It's the choreography," she remarked. "It's really jazzy and fresh. Patty and Jade must have helped her with it."

"Should we be worried?" asked Jean, nibbling her fingernails nervously. "I mean, what if they're not just good—what if they're better?"

Heather sniffed. "I have to give Jessica credit for making passable cheerleaders out of that motley crew. They are good, but they're not better. Besides"—a gloating smile wreathed her face—"I know something Jessica doesn't know."

"What's that?" asked Amy.

"There's a rule that only one team from each school can go to regionals," Heather replied, "and we've already been picked to represent Sweet Valley!"

"Phew!" Amy exclaimed, relieved. "For a minute there I was starting to sweat."

Jessica's squad was forming a pyramid. Heather watched, still smirking as she waited for them to lose their balance and tumble to the ground.

They didn't fall, but Heather decided it didn't matter. What good was a perfect pyramid going to do them? "It's really too bad they've wasted so much time," she drawled dismissively, snapping her gum as she turned her back on Jessica's squad. "Boy, is Jessica going to be burned when she finds out her team isn't even eligible for regionals!"

It was pitiful, really, that Jessica had even tried to start a new squad, decided Heather. Clearly Jessica just hadn't gotten the message yet. She wasn't the most popular girl at Sweet Valley High anymore—she wasn't the one setting the pace, the fashion. It was Heather's turn.

Chapter 7

"What do you mean, only one squad from a school can enter the regional cheerleading competition?" Jessica said to Lila over the phone on Saturday morning.

Still dressed in her robe and slippers, Jessica had been standing at the sink rinsing her cereal bowl when the phone rang. Now, holding the receiver between her ear and shoulder, she turned off the water and dried her hands on a dish towel.

"Just what I said. Only one squad can go per school—or to put it another way, each school is allowed to sponsor only one squad as its official representative. It's right here on page twenty-two of the ACA rule book."

"That can't be right," Jessica exclaimed. "It's not fair!"

"Rules aren't always fair," Lila pointed out. "I wouldn't have stumbled upon it myself if Heather dearest hadn't called a few minutes ago to casually suggest that I check out page twenty-two."

Jessica stamped her foot. "She is just so darned cocky, isn't she? She's so sure she can just laugh at us, that we're not a threat. I'm calling Mr. Jenkins."

"The American Cheerleading Association scout?"

"Yep. Maybe they don't enforce this particular rule, or maybe I can talk him into making an exception. He lives in Palisades, right?"

"Bridgewater, I think."

As soon as she hung up on Lila, Jessica dialed Bridgewater information. Elizabeth strolled into the room while Jessica was jotting Mr. Jenkins's number down.

"I'm calling Mr. Jenkins," Jessica informed her sister. "Wish me luck!"

A moment later she was speaking with the ACA scout who'd been so impressed with Heather and the rest of the Sweet Valley High squad at the game a week ago. "Mr. Jenkins, I'd like to find out about arranging an audition with you," Jessica announced. "My name is Jessica Wakefield, and I'm the captain of a new cheer squad at Sweet Valley High."

Elizabeth watched with interest as Jessica shook her head. "I was on Heather Mallone's squad—I mean, that was my squad! But I'm not anymore—I've formed my own team."

Now Jessica was nodding. "That's right. We're just getting started, but we're great, I don't mind saying. We have a really unique look and style, and I think you'll agree we're better than Heather's squad and we should be the ones representing Sweet Valley High at regionals—"

For a moment Jessica was silent while Mr. Jenkins talked. Then she burst out, "But if you'd just come to Sweet Valley and take a look. . . . I understand. I'm sorry, too. Good-bye."

Jessica replaced the receiver, her jaw clenched tight. "He didn't buy it, huh?" guessed Elizabeth.

"He said he's very busy scouting all the schools in the area." Jessica heaved a frustrated sigh. "He already visited SVH once and he doesn't plan on returning."

Elizabeth took a carton of orange juice from the refrigerator and gave it a shake before pouring herself a glass. "So he didn't say it was impossible for your squad to go in place of Heather's," she observed. "It was more a question of his not going to the trouble to check us out and make a comparison."

"Same difference."

Elizabeth tilted her head to one side. "Is it?"

"What are you getting at?"

Elizabeth shrugged. "I don't know. I guess I'm just surprised that you'd give up so easily. Maybe this isn't that important to you, after all."

"But it is!" Jessica cried. "I'd do anything to go to regionals, but what's the point if I can't get an audience with Mr. Jenkins?"

Elizabeth sipped her juice. "Like I said, I'm just surprised that you're giving up so easily."

Jessica stared at her sister. Then, slowly, a light brightened behind her eyes. She snapped her fingers. "I've got an idea!"

Elizabeth smiled. "I was wondering when your scheming brain would shift into high gear."

"Run upstairs and put on your cheerleading uniform," Jessica ordered, "while I call the rest of the squad."

"What's the plan?" asked Elizabeth.

Her sister grinned. "If the regional scout won't come to Jessica Wakefield, Jessica Wakefield will just have to go to the regional scout!"

"Mrs. Jenkins?" Jessica said to the attractive thirty-something woman who answered the front door of the stucco ranch house in Bridgewater.

Jessica was wearing her red-and-white cheerleading uniform; the rest of the squad, also in uniform and with pom-poms in hand, were lined up on the walk behind her. Mrs. Jenkins blinked at the sight. "Yes?"

"Is Mr. Jenkins home?" Jessica inquired.

"He's gone out to do a few errands," Mrs. Jenkins replied. "He should be back any minute, though. Can I help you?"

"Oh, no, thanks," said Jessica with a sweet smile. "But if it's OK, we'll just wait for him. Outside," she added quickly, smothering a giggle when she saw Mrs. Jenkins's look of horror at the prospect of having eight cheerleaders in her living room.

"That's fine," Mrs. Jenkins said, visibly relieved. "Have a nice—"

She started to close the door. "One more thing," Jessica called after her. "What kind of car does your husband drive?"

94

Mrs. Jenkins wrinkled her forehead, puzzled. "It's a red Honda Civic. Now if you'll excuse me . . ."

Hopping down from the front stoop, Jessica hustled her cheerleaders onto the Jenkinses' lawn. "He'll be home any minute," she informed the squad, "so as soon as we see a red Honda Civic, I want everyone to—"

"Look!" Maria pointed up the street. "I think that's him now!"

"All right, let's go!" shouted Jessica, hitting a button on the tape player and snatching up her pom-poms. "You know what we have to do!"

In a flash Maria, Sandy, and Elizabeth had boosted Patty and Sara onto their shoulders; Jessica and Lila then helped Jade scramble to the top. An impressive standing pyramid greeted Mr. Jenkins as he pulled into the driveway.

Flanking the pyramid, Jessica and Lila started stamping their feet and chanting. "We've got the beat and our team's got the heat. We will defeat any rivals we meet. . . ."

Mr. Jenkins had climbed out of his parked car and was standing at the edge of the lawn, grocery bags in his arms, watching Jessica and her squad perform. Bending quickly, Jessica cranked up the volume on the tape player.

The tempo of the music grew faster and more electrifying. Jade, Patty, and Sara had hopped down from the pyramid, and now the whole line of girls was whirling and leaping in turn. The routine built to its climax. In pairs the girls darted forward to perform their final stunts: Lila and Jade did no-hands cartwheels, landing in splits; Maria and Sandy did round-off, back handsprings; Sara and Patty each did a flip, one front and one back, and then shot into the air again in perfect stag leaps; and finally Jessica and Elizabeth did spread-eagles, landing front and center in side-by-side Chinese splits.

Mr. Jenkins put down the grocery bags so he could applaud. "Bravo!" he yelled, whistling. "Good show!"

Jessica hopped to her feet and trotted over to him, panting from the exertion. The other girls pressed close behind her. "What did you think, honestly?" Jessica asked with an eager smile after introducing herself.

"It's a dazzling routine," said Mr. Jenkins. "Highly technical and very original."

"I've incorporated some modern-dance choreography into it," said Jessica. "I think it makes us one of a kind."

"And I like the twin factor," he continued, beaming at the Wakefield sisters. Jessica elbowed Elizabeth in the ribs. "Yes, all in all this is one of the most impressive routines I've seen all season."

"So you'll give us a slot in regionals?" Jessica concluded, her eyes shining.

Mr. Jenkins's smile faded. "I'm afraid not," he said regretfully. "We've been over this, Jessica— you know the rules. Only one team from a school can compete, and although your squad is terrific, I've already granted a spot to Heather's squad. They earned it."

"They stole it," Jessica muttered under her breath. "It should have been ours!"

Mr. Jenkins patted her on the shoulder, then bent to retrieve his groceries. "Try again next year, girls," he called before disappearing into the house.

Jessica hurled her pom-poms onto the grass, her face crumpling. Elizabeth slipped an arm around her sister's shoulders. Lila, Maria, Sandy, Jade, Patty, and Sara all looked at each other, their eyes shadowed with disappointment.

"I'm—I'm sorry," Jessica stuttered, putting a hand to her eyes to dash away the tears. "I led you guys to think we could go all the way, and now it turns out we're not going any further than Mr. Jenkins's front yard. I wasted your time. I'm really, really sorry."

Her shoulders drooping and her chin on her chest, Jessica trudged toward the Jeep, alone.

"What a bummer," said Sara, her sigh weighted with disappointment. "Poor Jessica. She really had her heart set on this, didn't she?"

The eight girls were driving back to Sweet Valley; Lila, Maria, and Sandy were in the Jeep with Jessica, while Elizabeth, Sara, and Jade rode in Patty's Chevy Nova.

The Jeep was leading, but Jessica, usually a speedy driver, was setting a funeral-procession pace. "She staked all her hopes on going to regionals," agreed Elizabeth. "She didn't want to feel that Heather had beaten her, you know? She wanted

97

another chance to compete with her, on neutral ground. But I guess now she's going to have to hang up her pom-poms once and for all."

"It's really a shame," declared Patty, flipping on her turn signal as they neared an intersection. "I mean, I'll be the first to admit it—I was totally skeptical when she first approached me about cheering. But this past week I've really come to appreciate how demanding a sport it is. Not to mention fun!"

"I feel like I've really been stretched in new ways," agreed Jade. "I loved having a chance to get creative with my dance training, athleticize it, you know? Until I started cheerleading practice this week, I really had no idea how strong I was, how much I was capable of."

Elizabeth, sitting in the backseat, rested her arms on the seat in front of her. "I guess there's not much any of us can do but wait until next year, like Mr. Jenkins said. Maybe Jessica will find a way to get some kind of official status for her squad, or maybe you guys could try out for Heather's squad."

Sara wrinkled her nose. "I would never cheer for Heather," she pronounced.

"Her whole philosophy is based on excluding people," said Jade, "whereas Jessica really reached out to bring a whole new range of talents into her squad."

Elizabeth nodded. "That's true. In the past the cheerleaders were a pretty tight group. We've cracked the clique wide open!"

"Yeah, well," said Patty, reaching down to the

radio to give the dial a spin, "easy come, easy go."

Patty had tuned in to a local station. A game was being broadcast. "The SVH football game against El Carro!" Elizabeth realized, leaning forward to hear.

"I guess while we cheered for Mr. Jenkins, Heather and her squad were cheering for the Gladiators," said Sara.

"What's the score?" asked Jade.

The four girls listened until the announcer said, "As the first half winds down, the Gladiators have fallen behind twenty-eight to six. It looks like it's going to be a romp for El Carro High."

Patty turned off the radio in disgust. "They're getting trounced."

"Watch out!" Elizabeth cried.

Ahead of them Jessica had braked suddenly. Patty skidded to a halt, nearly rear-ending the Jeep. "What the—" she exclaimed.

Now Jessica was signaling, about to pull into the parking lot of a convenience store. Lila hung out the passenger-side window, beckoning urgently for Patty to follow.

"What's going on?" Jade wondered.

"Let's find out," said Patty, trailing the Jeep into the parking lot.

As soon as the Jeep was parked, Jessica, Lila, Maria, and Sandy poured out. They were quickly joined by Elizabeth and the others.

"You guys ready for another performance?" Jessica asked.

"What are you talking about?" said Elizabeth.

"The football game," explained Jessica. "Were you listening?"

"Sweet Valley's losing," said Patty. "There doesn't seem to be much point in stopping by for the second half."

"We're all going to stop by," Jessica told her. "The Gladiators could use our help."

"What are you talking about?" Elizabeth repeated.

Jessica grinned. "I'm talking about cheerleading. I'm talking about how we've practiced hard all week and now it's time to show the world what we can do!"

"You want us to go down to the field and perform?" said Elizabeth in disbelief.

Jessica nodded. "We're in uniform and we're all warmed up," she pointed out. "What's to stop us?"

The other girls began buzzing excitedly. Only Elizabeth protested. "But, Jess, we can't do that! We're not the real squad!"

"Oh, no?" Jessica lifted her chin, her eyes flashing with pride and determination. "I think we should let the fans decide. C'mon!" She waved the girls back to the cars. "It's almost halftime—we'd better hurry!"

Jessica was already settling into the driver's seat of the Jeep, revving the engine. Elizabeth had no choice but to pile back into Patty's Nova. She found her heart racing with anticipation. *This is the real thing,* Elizabeth thought, sparked by Jessica's fire. *We're going to cheer in front of the whole school!*

The stands at the football field were packed with fans, but the mood, on the Sweet Valley side at least, was solemn. "We're just in time," Jessica hissed as she and the other girls darted under the home-team bleachers. "Only one minute till halftime. Stay right here, and don't let anyone see you!"

Jessica had put on a denim jacket over her cheerleading uniform. Donning dark sunglasses as well, she jogged quickly up the steps and ducked into the sound booth at the top of the stands. The announcer, busy recapping highlights of the game so far, didn't even notice her. The girl sitting in front of the broadcasting controls, however, waved Jessica to a halt. "Hey, what are you doing in here?"

"There's been a change," Jessica said breathlessly. "The cheerleading music, at halftime?" Taking a cassette from her jacket pocket, she pressed it into the girl's hand. "Play this instead."

"Are you sure?" the girl asked. "Who authorized—"

"Just play it," Jessica said firmly. "It'll be all right, I promise."

Before the girl could ask any more questions, Jessica dashed back out of the booth.

Underneath the bleachers she found her squad huddled in a tight knot. "All of a sudden I'm really nervous," Jade confessed.

"We've never performed in front an audience before," said Sara, her teeth chattering.

101

"What if we forget our moves?" wondered Patty.

"You won't forget—you'll be brilliant," Jessica declared, bundling them into a big hug. Elizabeth proffered the canvas equipment bag, and Jessica reached in to hand pom-poms all around. "When the music starts . . ." She looked upward, her lips moving in a rapid prayer. "And please, please let it start. . . . When it starts, just let out all the stops. Go for it. We've got nothing to lose!"

They all turned to face the football field through the slats of the bleachers. The scoreboard was in plain view as the last seconds of the first half ticked down. "Ten, nine, eight, seven, six," Jessica murmured, her heart beginning to thump like a kettledrum. "Five, four, three, two, one. That's our cue!"

The two football teams started to trot off the field. On the opposite side of the field, the El Carro cheerleaders were getting ready to perform. Heather and her squad bent to retrieve their pom-poms, brushed dust off their skirts, smoothed their hair.

As Jessica's squad stormed the field, she heard a murmur start up in the stands. Then the music started: her music, the tape she'd put together with Patty and Jade's help.

Before Heather had time to react, Jessica's squad was lined up on the field facing the home-team bleachers. The Sweet Valley fans quickly figured out what they were seeing and began hooting their approval. The squad launched straight into their routine, smiling at the crowd and yelling at the top of their lungs. "We've got the beat and our team's got the heat," Jessica shouted. "We will defeat any rivals we meet!"

The music had a jazzy, irresistible rhythm. Jessica's squad clapped energetically, and soon the fans were clapping with them. The sound was deafening.

One by one, Jessica and her team performed their dazzling airborne combinations. Each time one of the girls landed a jump, the crowd roared. By the time the routine reached its stirring climax, the fans were on their feet, waving banners and tossing confetti.

Jessica landed her last jump and sank to the earth in a split. The squad held their pose while the audience applauded wildly. The Sweet Valley High football team had jogged back onto the field to watch the performance; to Jessica's delight, Ken had seen it all. But that was nothing compared to the satisfaction she got from watching Heather's reaction.

For the first time since she'd moved to Sweet Valley, confident, beautiful Heather Mallone appeared to be at a total loss. She stood on the sidelines, her squad lined up behind her, pom-poms on her hips and her mouth hanging open. Jessica grinned and waved at the crowd, blowing kisses and laughing. *Mirror, mirror on the wall,* she thought, giddy with triumph. *Now who's got the fairest cheerleading squad of all?*

✿ ✿ ✿

As usual, the Dairi Burger was packed to the rafters after the football game. When Jessica walked in with Ken, they were immediately besieged by friends. "Really awesome, Wakefield!" boomed Bruce Patman, planting a kiss on Jessica's cheek and then slugging Ken playfully in the shoulder.

"You guys were great," echoed Bruce's girlfriend, Pamela Robertson. "You should be out there all the time!"

"Weren't they fantastic?" Ken agreed, his arm firmly around Jessica's shoulders. "I've always thought cheerleaders played an important role, but I never realized they could do that much to fire a team up."

"The final score tells the whole story," said Scottie Trost, the Gladiators' wide receiver. "Thirty-four to twenty-eight—what a comeback!"

Jessica beamed. "Well, we can't take all the credit," she said modestly. "You guys played a great game."

"I'm telling you, we couldn't have done it without you," Ken insisted, giving her a big kiss. "Seeing you back on the field, Jess—it was just like old times."

"It was better than old times," declared Todd, giving Elizabeth a squeeze. "Thanks to all the new talent Jessica recruited!"

The moment was perfect . . . until Amy, who'd been huddled in a booth with her boyfriend, Barry Rork, charged over to Jessica. "How could you do that to us?" she demanded tearfully.

104

"Heather didn't give me much of a choice—besides, she did it to me first," replied Jessica. "You said it yourself the other day, Amy—nothing personal, right?"

"It is personal. You made me look like an idiot in front of the whole school!"

Jessica smiled. "So how did it feel?"

Amy shook her head. "I can't believe you're taking pleasure in this." A tear streaked down her cheek. "I guess this means we're not friends anymore!"

Before Jessica could reason with her, Amy bolted from the restaurant. Jessica shrugged. Amy's outburst had tarnished the moment, but only slightly. As more and more people poured into the Dairi Burger, Jessica continued to be surrounded by admiring schoolmates and barraged with compliments. Everyone preferred her squad to Heather's, no contest. Heather, meanwhile, was nowhere to be seen—as soon as the game ended, she'd headed home in a sulk.

"So is it true, Jessica?" Zack Johnson, a Gladiators' linebacker, wanted to know. "Are you guys really the new squad? Are you taking over from Heather?"

"Well, I don't know," said Jessica coyly. "Do you think we should?"

The answer was a resounding "yes." All around her Jessica's friends were toasting her with milk shakes and soft drinks. "Here's to Jessica, Liz, Lila, Maria, Sandy, Jade, Patty, and Sara," said Ken, his blue eyes glowing with love and pride. "The best

105

cheerleaders in the history of Sweet Valley High!"

The praise was like candy; Jessica couldn't get enough of it. *I'm back where I belong,* she thought happily, remembering the day Heather Mallone had walked into the Dairi Burger and begun the process of trying to elbow Jessica out of her place at the top of the SVH social hierarchy.

She had the winning quarterback at her side; they were the couple of the hour. Yes, Jessica was back in the spotlight. Now she just had to make sure she stayed there.

Chapter 8

At the start of lunch period on Monday, Jessica hurried straight to the principal's office. As usual, Rosemary, Mr. Cooper's secretary, was barricading the door like a dragon guarding a treasure trove. *Like anyone actually wants to go in there!* Jessica thought.

Rosemary peered at Jessica through her bifocals. "Do you have an appointment, dear?"

"No, but I need to speak to . . ." Jessica caught herself just in time from saying "Chrome Dome," the student body's irreverent nickname for the bald principal. ". . . to Mr. Cooper as soon as possible. Make that immediately, as in right now. It's extremely urgent!"

Rosemary raised her wispy, overplucked eyebrows. "Well, let me see if he can squeeze you in before his appointment in the faculty lunch room," she offered in a grudging tone, as if she were doing

Jessica the biggest favor in the history of the world.

Rosemary buzzed Mr. Cooper and mumbled something incoherent. Then she looked at Jessica, her head bobbing on her skinny neck. "The principal will see you now," she said formally.

Circling Rosemary's desk, Jessica pushed open the door to Chrome Dome Cooper's office. "Hi, Mr. Cooper," she said cheerfully.

"Jessica, it's good to see you." The round-faced principal stood up and waved her into a chair facing his desk. "What can I do for you today?"

Jessica sat down, folding her hands on her lap. "It's about cheerleading, sir."

"Ah." Seated again, Chrome Dome propped his elbows on the desk and tented his fingers under his double chin. "Cheerleading."

"As you may know, I quit the varsity squad about ten days ago because of . . . personality differences with Heather Mallone, the new cocaptain," Jessica explained. "I decided to form my own squad, and all last week we practiced like crazy. We knew the old squad—Heather's squad—was going to regionals, and we thought we could go, too. But it turns out that only one team per school can go."

"Oh, that's too bad, too bad," clucked Chrome Dome.

"The thing is, Mr. Cooper," said Jessica, leaning forward in her chair. Suddenly her eyes were blazing. "It's not fair that Heather's squad should automatically get to go to regionals. The cheerleading competition is about school spirit, and I think my squad has more of that. She formed her team by kicking people out—I formed mine by inviting people in. And I just know that if the student body could vote on which squad they want to represent them at regionals, mine would win hands down!"

It was a stirring speech and Chrome Dome was clearly affected. "Well, I'll tell you, Jessica," he said, rubbing his bald head until it was shinier than ever, "I was at the game on Saturday, and I thought your squad was terrific, just terrific. Now, that's not to say I approved of your just bursting onto the scene without getting permission first, but on the other hand, the fans loved it, they definitely loved it. The team loved it—they turned the tables on El Carro and pulled off a victory. Yes, it showed school spirit all right—clearly you girls have plenty of that."

"So you think it's a good idea?" Jessica asked eagerly. "Having the whole school vote?"

"I think it's an excellent idea," he confirmed, thumping a fist on his desk for emphasis, "a very sound, democratic idea. Yes, the students should vote, because, after all, it should be their cheerleading squad competing at regionals—not yours or Heather's but Sweet Valley High's."

"I couldn't agree more," declared Jessica.

"We'll have a—what shall we call it?—a cheer-off tomorrow," Mr. Cooper suggested. "Both teams can display their talents in front of the entire student body. After school, of course."

"Of course!" Jessica agreed, springing to her feet. "Oh, thanks, Mr. Cooper. Thanks so much!"

In her joy she was almost tempted to kiss old Chrome Dome on his polished pink head. Almost.

"I think 'The Pom-pom Wars' story came out great," Penny said to Elizabeth before the *Oracle* staff meeting got started during lunch period. "Do you think you could do a follow-up story? I mean, it was so exciting, the way Jessica's squad charged onto the field at halftime of the football game on Saturday. Personally, I always thought the cheerleaders were just there for decoration, but that performance changed my mind."

Hitching herself onto a table, Elizabeth swung her feet, kicking them against the table legs. "I'm afraid the follow-up would be kind of anticlimactic," she replied. "The pom-pom wars seem to be over. Heather's team won."

Elizabeth told Penny about the unsuccessful visit to the ACA scout's home. "He told us to try again next year. Jessica was pretty bummed, as you might expect. She felt better after that halftime stunt, but I don't see how it can change anything. Heather's squad is going to regionals and we're not—that's the bottom line."

At that moment Mr. Collins entered the room, and Elizabeth and Penny turned their attention to him. The meeting was brief—Mr. Collins reviewed some upcoming deadlines and then demonstrated a few additional tricks for using INFOMAX, the new on-line computer database. Elizabeth took some notes and asked a couple of questions. As soon as the meeting was over, the other students disappeared, eager to get to the cafeteria to grab a bite before the bell rang. Only Elizabeth stayed behind, experimenting with INFOMAX.

Mr. Collins had taken a seat at a desk in order to look over the first draft of a feature article for Olivia Davidson, the *Oracle*'s arts editor. When Elizabeth turned off her computer a few minutes later and got to her feet, he smiled across the room at her. "I wanted to congratulate you on your new-found talent, Liz." He smiled, the corners of his sky-blue eyes crinkling. "Teddy and I were at the game on Saturday, and we were both very impressed. Teddy couldn't wait to boast to his friends that not only does his favorite baby-sitter tell the best stories, but she can do cartwheels and back flips, too!"

Elizabeth laughed. Mr. Collins, one of her favorite teachers at Sweet Valley High, was a divorced single parent, and she often baby-sat for his six-year-old son. "I have to admit I was having a blast out there," she confessed. "It's really a fun sport—I'm starting to see why Jessica's so into it."

"Just don't overdo it," Mr. Collins cautioned. "I don't want you showing up with a sprained wrist or something."

"I'd type with my toes if I had to," Elizabeth joked. "Anything to get the story out!"

Mr. Collins tipped his chair backward and gazed at her, his smile more thoughtful. "I've been meaning to talk to you about something, Liz—something else. Remember that story you told me about your friend, the one who fell for her boyfriend's best friend when her boyfriend was out of town?"

Elizabeth felt a blush crawl up her neck to her face. "Um, yeah. What—what about it?"

"Well, I was wondering if your friend had any luck resolving the issue."

"Actually . . ." Elizabeth ducked her head, hiding behind a curtain of blond hair. "Actually, I'd say if anything, the situation is worse. You see, my friend's girlfriend, the one who's dating the other guy now, found out that my friend used to be involved with her—the second girl's—new boyfriend. Are you following me?"

"I think so," said Mr. Collins. "So, what happened?"

"Nothing, really. But now my friend's more confused than ever. She's still thinking about that other guy, but at the same time she's also incredibly worried that her boyfriend will find out about what happened in the past."

"What tangled webs we weave, eh?" said Mr. Collins, raking a hand through his strawberry-blond hair. "This is the thing, Liz. You asked for my advice . . . for your friend . . . but later I realized I left out the most important part. The honesty-is-the-best-policy part."

"Oh, that," Elizabeth said wryly.

Mr. Collins smiled. "It's a pretty useful all-purpose moral to just about any story," he remarked. "My point in this case is that your friend has a pretty compelling reason to do the right thing. If she doesn't tell her boyfriend about the other guy, the guilt is going to eat her alive."

Immediately Elizabeth felt the truth of Mr. Collins's words in the depths of her heart. *He's right—I am being eaten alive,* she thought.

"Honesty is the best policy," Elizabeth said softly. "Thanks, Mr. Collins. I'll discuss this with my friend right away. It'll be hard, but she'll just have to find a way to bring it up with her boyfriend. He might get upset, but down the road their relationship will be stronger, right? I mean, because they were honest with each other?"

"There's no guarantee, but perhaps he'll understand," said Mr. Collins. "The important thing is, she'll be able to live with herself."

"Right." Elizabeth put a hand on the doorknob, then turned back. "Thanks. Or did I say that already?"

"It's nothing." Mr. Collins lifted his hands, smiling. "Free advice, all day, any day."

Elizabeth laughed. "See ya, Mr. Collins."

"Take it easy, Liz."

As she walked down the corridor toward the cafeteria, Elizabeth mulled over Mr. Collins's wise words. *Honesty is the best policy,* she repeated to herself, trying to work up her courage to confront Todd. She'd do it that very afternoon—they had a date to go out for pizza. *Honesty is the best policy, honesty is the best policy . . .*

As Elizabeth approached the swinging door to the cafeteria, the loudspeaker system crackled. The vice principal briskly ran through the usual array of lunchtime announcements, and then there was some static and Chrome Dome himself came on the air. Elizabeth stopped in her tracks to listen.

"Ahem, I have one additional piece of news to share with you," Mr. Cooper said, clearing his throat. "Tomorrow after school there will be a special assembly in the gym. The entire student body is invited to view routines performed by the two cheerleading squads captained by Heather Mallone and Jessica Wakefield, respectively, and then to vote on which squad should represent Sweet Valley High at the regionals competition."

Chrome Dome's remaining words were drowned out by the uproar in the cafeteria. Elizabeth pushed into the crowded lunchroom; the din of voices was deafening.

"Is it true?" students were demanding of each other. "A cheer-off? Wow, cool, what a great idea!"

"I'm for Jessica's squad one hundred percent," Elizabeth heard someone say.

"No way, Heather's squad is much better," another voice argued. "She's in a class by herself—she's dynamite."

Everyone had an opinion. "Kicking Maria and Sandy off the squad—that was her first mistake." "I really hope this puts her in her place." "But what makes Jessica think she can just take over the whole way sports are run at SVH?" "Her squad was better, though. Don't those girls deserve a shot at the championship?"

"Jessica!" Elizabeth shouted when she spotted her twin.

Jessica waved happily. "Come on over here,

Liz," she called. "Help me out with this press conference!"

Once again Jessica was surrounded by schoolmates plying her with questions and compliments. Elizabeth stepped to her sister's side.

"It's pretty clear why we have an edge," Jessica told her fans, slipping an arm around Elizabeth's waist. "The old squad used to have one Wakefield twin, but now it has none—while my squad has two!"

Elizabeth rolled her eyes, laughing. "Modest as always," she teased Jessica.

"Hey, I have no regrets," Jessica said. "Modesty's not about to get us to regionals."

"Nothing will get you to regionals," a voice snapped harshly.

Elizabeth and Jessica both whirled. Heather had marched up behind them. Bright spots of color stood out on her fair cheeks; Elizabeth almost expected to see steam shoot from her ears.

"Oh, good, Heather, there you are," said Jessica, her tone silky smooth. "You know, I just love that dress—I saw the exact same one at Lisette's, but I didn't buy it because I didn't think the color would be good on a blonde. Anyhow, Mr. Cooper wants to meet with the two of us to talk about the procedure for the cheer-off tomorrow. Can you spare a few minutes before practice this afternoon?"

"Do I have a choice?" Heather spat out angrily.

"Sure, you have a choice," said Jessica with a playful grin. "You could choose to boycott the cheer-off—to forfeit. Then my squad could save our energy for regionals!"

"Forget it," declared Heather. "We'll be at the cheer-off, and we'll prove to the whole world that you're just looking for attention. You don't have the real stuff. You don't have what it takes to win at regionals, but we do."

"I guess our fellow students will decide, won't they?" said Jessica with admirable coolness.

"They'll decide, and you'll be sorry," Heather predicted, turning on her heel and flouncing off.

Elizabeth and Jessica stared after Heather. Then they looked at one another and burst out laughing. "A week ago I would have been scared to death of that girl," said Jessica, "but not anymore. I think she's starting to show her true colors, and finally I'm not the only one who's able to see them!"

"What is it, Liz?" asked Enid on Monday afternoon. "You sounded frantic on the phone, so I drove as fast as I could."

In half an hour Todd would be picking up Elizabeth for their pizza date. After much agonizing Elizabeth had decided she couldn't go through with her honesty-is-the-best-policy plan without practicing her confession first.

Now she ushered Enid into the front hall. "Thanks for dropping everything to come over," said Elizabeth. "I can't tell you how much I appreciate it, you're just the best friend and I'd be lost without you—"

116

Enid held up a hand. "Whoa, Liz, you're bab-
bling. Slow down!"

Elizabeth took a deep breath. "OK, let's—I
think Jessica is out back by the pool. Let's go upstairs."

She led the way to her bedroom. Once inside,
she closed and locked the door. Enid laughed.
"Liz, you're acting like you're about to brief me
about an undercover spy mission. What's going
on?"

Enid sat down on the edge of Elizabeth's bed;
Elizabeth perched on the desk chair. "I have to tell
you something," Elizabeth began, "that I would
have told you a long time ago, except I decided not
to tell anyone. We decided. But now I realize I
should have told someone in particular—Todd, not
you—but before I tell him, I thought I'd tell you."

She paused to take a breath and realized her
hands were shaking. "Liz, you're not making
sense," Enid said, her voice soothing. "Start at the
beginning, OK?"

"OK." Elizabeth's eyes shifted to the desk
drawer where the diary was hidden. *I could just let
her read it,* she thought somewhat illogically. *I
could just let everyone read it—we could print ex-
cerpts in* The Oracle!

"It started when Todd moved to Vermont,"
Elizabeth related. "Remember how lonely I was? I
thought I'd die without him. And then after a while
I realized I was going to make it, but I was pretty
sure I'd never find another boy to love for as long
as I lived."

"I remember," said Enid with an encouraging smile. "You met Jeffrey, though, and then Todd moved back. So you weren't lonely forever."

Elizabeth nodded. "But before Todd moved back, before Jeffrey . . ." She gulped; her voice dropped to a whisper. "There was someone else."

Enid gaped. "Someone else? You're kidding!"

"I wish I were," said Elizabeth.

"Who?"

Elizabeth counted to ten in her head. She knew Enid was going to fall off the bed when she heard this. "Ken Matthews."

Enid did practically topple over with astonishment. "Ken Matthews?" she repeated, her voice a surprised squeak. "But no one ever—how did you—where—when—I can't believe it!"

"We were really careful," Elizabeth explained. "We steered clear of each other in school, and all our 'dates' were to places no one was likely to spot us. It was a secret from everybody."

"Because you were still Todd's girlfriend, and Ken was Todd's best friend," said Enid.

Elizabeth nodded glumly. "So do you despise me?"

"Oh, of course not." Enid's eyes were warm with sympathy. "Things like that happen, you know? Todd dated other girls while he lived in Vermont—he was open about that."

"That's just it," exclaimed Elizabeth. "He was open and I wasn't. At least I wasn't open about Ken. I told Todd about my dates with Nicholas Morrow and later about Jeffrey, but Ken . . . that

118

was different. I knew he'd be crushed."

"So even after he moved back to Sweet Valley and you two started going out again, you didn't tell him," Enid deduced.

Elizabeth shook her head. "At that point I figured what he didn't know couldn't hurt him." She laughed humorlessly. "Now, *there's* a motto for people who don't buy into the 'honesty is the best policy' philosophy!"

"And now it's bothering you," said Enid, "and you think you should come clean with Todd."

"It is bothering me." Elizabeth twisted a strand of hair around her right index finger. "But it's complicated, because it's bothering me for a bunch of different reasons in a bunch of different ways."

Enid's eyes glittered with sudden understanding. "Oh, I see," she said. "Jessica and Ken! You're not jealous, are you?"

Elizabeth decided now wasn't the time to go into all the pathetic details of her current emotional crisis. "'Jealousy' isn't really the right word," she said evasively. "Jessica found out about me and Ken—that's basically what got me rethinking all of this."

"She found out and she didn't kill you?" Enid asked in amazement. "What I mean is, she found out and she didn't immediately blab to everybody in Sweet Valley?"

"Doesn't sound like Jessica, does it?" agreed Elizabeth with a grim smile. "I bet this sounds like Jessica, though."

She told Enid about Jessica's blackmailing

strategy. Enid slapped her hand on the bed. "I knew there had to be some weird reason why you decided to join Jessica's squad! Boy, that's low. That's really low!"

"It's no worse than I deserve," said Elizabeth, "and the upside is that I don't hate cheerleading as much as I expected to. If nothing else, it's great exercise. But the whole mess made me realize that this secret isn't good for my mental health. So when Todd and I go out tonight . . ."

Enid reached forward to pat Elizabeth on the knee. "It's the right thing to do, Liz. I'm behind you all the way."

Just thinking about the scene with Todd made Elizabeth want to throw up. "Do you think he'll be mad? What if he storms out of Guido's Pizza Palace? What if he decides he never wants to see me again?"

Elizabeth was on the verge of hysterical tears. "Calm down," Enid advised. "I bet anything it won't happen that way. He'll be shocked, sure, and hurt. He may need to take some time to himself to think about it, figure out how he feels. But then he'll realize that in the grand scheme of things, it's just kind of a blip."

"A blip."

"Right, a blip. The fact is, it didn't amount to anything between you and Ken. You went back to being just friends. And your motives for keeping the whole thing from Todd were pretty pure—you didn't want to hurt his feelings."

Pretty pure—I doubt that! thought Elizabeth.

But she wanted to see the situation the way Enid did. "If the roles were reversed," she said, "if I moved away and Todd went out with you, and then I found out about it a million years later . . ." She wrinkled her nose. "I don't know how I'd feel."

Enid laughed. "You've obviously been thinking too much about this, and now we're talking it to death. You'll psyche yourself out. Just do it."

Enid gave Elizabeth's hand a reaffirming squeeze. Elizabeth made her mind go blank, and then she let one simple idea enter. *I'll tell Todd and then it will all be over,* she thought.

She nodded, feeling strengthened by Enid's support and her own inner resolve. "I will," she declared. "I'll do it."

"You're really packing away that pizza," Todd observed an hour later as they sat opposite each other in a booth at Guido's Pizza Palace. "I'm glad we ordered a large!"

"We had a grueling practice this afternoon," said Elizabeth, reaching for another thick slice of the Guido's special. "As you can imagine, Jessica isn't taking the slightest chance of losing the cheer-off tomorrow. We ran through our routine about a hundred times."

"Speaking of the cheer-off," said Todd, reaching for another piece of pizza himself, "Winston, Ken, and I were talking, and we thought maybe we'd make flyers and banners promoting your squad." He grinned sheepishly. "Just a bunch of proud boy-friends demonstrating our support."

Elizabeth's spine stiffened at the mention of Ken's name, especially in the context of "boyfriends." She managed to crack a weak smile. "That's really . . . sweet."

"Well, I can't speak for the other guys, but I'm always psyched to find a way to show you how much I love you."

"Oh, Todd," Elizabeth mumbled, dropping her eyes.

Quickly, she took a sip of her soda so he wouldn't see her chin tremble. *Oh, Todd . . . why do you have to make this so hard?*

Since arriving at the restaurant, she'd been waiting for an opportunity to bring up the subject of her and Ken. After talking with Enid, she'd felt pumped up and ready. She couldn't wait to have a clean slate with Todd, to free herself from the weight that had been settling more and more heavily upon her heart—and to free herself from Jessica. Once Todd knew everything, Jessica wouldn't have any power over her.

But so far the right moment hadn't presented itself. *I can't just say, "Pass the Parmesan—oh, and by the way, I was in love with your buddy Ken Matthews once."*

"Speak of the devil," said Todd, his eyes directed at a point behind Elizabeth. He waved. "Hey, Matthews, Jess. Over here."

Elizabeth turned, then groaned silently. Jessica and Ken were strolling toward their booth.

"What a surprise," Jessica said with a grin. "We didn't expect to see you."

"How's it going?" Ken asked.

"Pretty good. Have a seat," invited Todd.

"Sure, we'd be—" Ken started to say.

"Actually," Jessica interrupted, "you guys look like you're almost through." She winked broadly at her sister. "And I see a nice table for two by the waterfall that has our name on it. Catch you later."

As he passed the booth, Ken gave Todd a high five. Elizabeth sank back in her seat, swallowing her relief. What a close call. . . .

Todd was watching Ken and Jessica walk away. "You know," he said when the pair was out of ear-shot, "I don't really understand what Ken sees in Jessica, but I've got to say this much—she's really making him happy."

Elizabeth nodded dumbly. Only a blind person could have missed Ken and Jessica's starry-eyed glow, not to mention Jessica's slightly rumpled hair. They'd probably stopped at Miller's Point on their way over. . . .

"He's really in love—he finally met the right girl," continued Todd. "Can you believe it? I mean, the guy has dated a lot of girls, a lot of really cute, nice girls, too. But the other day he told me he'd only been in love once before."

"Once before, huh?" Elizabeth felt her face go pale and then flush hotly. She knew in her gut who that other girl was. *Once before . . . with me.*

"Nobody deserves more for something good to happen to him." Todd refilled their glasses from the pitcher of soda. "He's a great guy, you know? I'm pretty lucky to have a best friend like him."

"You are," Elizabeth murmured.

"I mean, I'd do anything for him, and I know he'd do anything for me." Todd looked straight into Elizabeth's eyes. "Loyalty. That's what friendship is all about, right?"

Elizabeth felt as if she'd been stripped naked, as if her soul lay bare and exposed on the table. But Todd didn't seem to see anything out of the ordinary; he was smiling at her. "Right," she said, her voice little more than a whisper.

She ate the rest of her pizza in silence, listening to Todd chat about possible banner slogans for the cheer-off. *I can't tell him*, she realized, the pizza she'd eaten sitting heavy as a stone in her stomach. *I can't tell him that his best friend, as well as his girlfriend, betrayed him in the worst way imaginable. God, how could I have thought even for a moment that that was the right thing to do?*

Elizabeth remembered Mr. Collins's comment when she'd filled him in on the latest installment of "her friend's" problem. "What tangled webs we weave. . . ."

The web was too tangled, and no matter how she looked at the situation, Elizabeth simply couldn't see a way to extricate herself. Her relationship with Todd wasn't the only thing at stake; there was also Todd and Ken's friendship to consider. And first and last, there were her stubbornly strong feelings for Ken. . . .

Enid had characterized Ken and Elizabeth's long-ago secret fling as a "blip," and Elizabeth hadn't bothered to argue the point. "When you

124

look at the big picture," Enid had said, "it's just not that important."

But a blip was something that came and went with no aftereffects, whereas Elizabeth's feelings for Ken had reasserted themselves until they were as all-consuming as anything else in the big picture of her life.

No, I absolutely can't under any circumstances tell him, Elizabeth concluded once and for all, gazing dismally across the table at Todd's cheerful, innocent face. *Sorry, Mr. Collins, but I guess I'm just going to have to be eaten alive!*

Chapter 9

At school on Tuesday morning Jessica tossed a few books into her locker and dug around for the notebook she needed for her first class. Then she slammed the locker door and plunged into the crowd of jostling students.

She couldn't help strutting just a little. The cheerleaders on both squads were wearing their uniforms, as was traditional the day of a big game, and she was pleasantly conscious that all eyes were on her in her short, perky red-and-white outfit. She walked along with a happy bounce. The cheer-off was still hours away, but already her leg muscles felt coiled, supple, strong. *When it comes to cheerleading, I'm the best there is,* she thought, brimming with confidence. *Heather may be hot, but I'm volcanic.*

"Jess. Jess, wait up!"

Jessica stepped out of the traffic and turned to

look behind her, an expectant smile on her face. Amy, also dressed in her cheerleading uniform, was hurrying toward her.

When she saw who had called out to her, the smile on Jessica's face faded. "Oh, it's you," she grumbled.

"Jessica, can we talk?" asked Amy, her own expression conciliatory.

Jessica shrugged. "Yes, I believe we both have the capability of speech," she said haughtily.

"Oh, don't be a pain, you know what I mean." Amy grabbed Jessica's arm and gave it a yank. "Just give me a chance to say one thing, OK?"

With a show of reluctance Jessica followed Amy into the girls' room. Once there, she folded her arms across her chest and lifted her chin, her manner completely unreceptive.

"You don't have to look so fierce," Amy began, tucking a strand of silky ash-blond hair behind one ear. "I just wanted to apologize."

Jessica blinked. "Apologize?"

Amy nodded. "I was really out of control at the Dairi Burger on Saturday night. I didn't mean what I said."

"You sure sounded like you meant it."

"It was the heat of the moment. I mean, you totally humiliated us. I was still feeling pretty burned. But afterward, when I thought about it for a while, I realized you were totally in the right. We deserved it."

"Well, Amy, that's very big of you to say so," observed Jessica graciously.

"Isn't it, though?" They smiled at each other. "The thing is, even though we're on rival squads, I want us to still be friends. I don't care if it ticks Heather off. I'll understand if you still have hard feelings toward me, but I want you to know I don't have any hard feelings toward you. In fact, I'm proud of you. It took a lot of gumption to go out there and form your own squad, and you guys are good. Not as good as us," she hurried to add, "but still, pretty darned good!"

Amy's slate-gray eyes sparkled with earnest tears; Jessica felt her own eyes grow moist. The two girls exchanged a quick hug. "Thanks, Amy," Jessica said, sniffling. "I can't tell you how much better I feel."

"Me, too." Amy fumbled in her purse for a tissue and blew her nose loudly. "It's really a relief to know that no matter who wins the cheer-off this afternoon, we'll still be friends."

"Right," said Jessica, although there was no doubt in her mind which squad was going to win the cheer-off . . . and reign supreme at Sweet Valley High forevermore. She grinned slyly. "And maybe if you're really nice to me, Amy, next year I'll let you try out for my squad!"

By lunchtime the entire school was decorated with streamers, balloons, posters, and pennants proclaiming the superior talent, beauty, and popularity of the two rival cheerleading squads. Amy's boyfriend, Barry Rork, and Annie's boyfriend, Tony Esteban, had printed up dozens of posters with a huge blowup picture of Heather and her squad; Todd, Ken, and Winston, meanwhile, were spearheading the "campaign" on behalf of Jessica's squad, with help from Sandy's boyfriend, Manuel, and Jade's boyfriend, David. They'd spent all night making buttons and banners urging the student body to "Send Jessica's team to Regionals!"

Elizabeth carried her tray through the cafeteria to an empty table, feeling almost embarrassed by the hoopla that had grown up around the cheer-off. *And having to wear this uniform to school!* she thought, glancing down at her long tanned legs emerging from underneath the very short, flirty skirt. *Unbelievable. Absolutely unbelievable!*

Enid stopped Elizabeth. "Liz, Jessica's waving to us," she told her friend. "There's a whole bunch of people sitting at a table over—"

"I don't think I'm up to it," Elizabeth cut in. "Is it OK with you if we steer clear of the fuss?"

"Sure, whatever you want," Enid said agreeably.

They sat at a small corner table, facing each other. "I was going to call you last night, to see how it went with Todd," Enid said, her fork poised over her plate of macaroni and cheese. "I saw you two together this morning before school, and you looked like normal. So everything's fine?"

Elizabeth squeezed a packet of low-cal dressing onto her chef's salad. "Everything's the same," she corrected her friend, making a wry face. "I chickened out. I didn't tell him about Ken."

"Oh, Liz. What happened?"

Elizabeth gave Enid a rundown of the previous

evening's scene at Guido's Pizza Palace. "I know what it's like to try to screw up your courage to initiate a conversation like that. Wouldn't you know Jess and Ken would walk in at just the wrong moment?" Enid commiserated.

"Maybe it was just the right moment," Elizabeth reflected. "Maybe it's better for some skeletons to stay in the closet, so to speak."

"I know you're concerned about hurting Todd's feelings, and you should be. But what about you?" asked Enid. "What about your peace of mind?"

Before Elizabeth could answer, somebody tapped her urgently on her shoulder. A moment later her twin sister was literally dragging her out of her chair. "Come on, Liz," chirped Jessica. "I need you!"

"What's going on?" Elizabeth demanded as Jessica pulled her through the cafeteria. Then she saw why Jessica "needed" her. "Oh, Jess," Elizabeth groaned. "Could you leave me out of this?"

"Leave you out of this? Are you kidding?" said Jessica. "Liz, you're part of the squad. You're one of our shining stars!"

A crowd had formed around a couple of tables that had been pushed together. All the trays had been cleared off, and in their place stood Lila, Maria, Sandy, Jade, Patty, and Sara. As the twins approached, the other girls began tapping their feet and clapping.

Jessica jumped lightly up onto the table, hauling Elizabeth after her. Then she cupped her hands around her mouth megaphone style. "We just wanted to make sure you're all getting psyched," she called out to the crowd.

There were cheers and whistles, as well as a few scattered boos from Heather supporters. Todd caught Elizabeth's eye and grinned proudly; Elizabeth tried to smile and look as if she were enjoying herself when in reality she wished she could crawl under the table and disappear.

"And that you're planning to come to the cheer-off and vote for your favorite cheerleaders!" Jessica continued.

The din grew louder. People started chanting Jessica's squad's signature cheer. "We've got the beat and our team's got the heat. . . ."

Jessica, in her element, started clapping and stamping along with her squad. Reluctantly, Elizabeth followed suit. After marching around the table waving a pro-Jessica banner, Winston grabbed some of the guys standing nearby and formed an impromptu all-male kick line. Someone released a bunch of red and white helium balloons. Elizabeth couldn't help laughing. She had to say one thing for the great cheer-off—it was shaping into one of the biggest events in recent Sweet Valley High history. *Maybe I'll be writing a follow-up article after all!* she thought.

The SVH gymnasium after school on Tuesday looked like halftime at the Super Bowl. The bleachers were packed with students waving banners and balloons; the air was snowy with confetti. On opposite sides of the basketball court, the two cheerleading squads were warming up.

As Jessica stretched her Achilles tendons and then lowered herself carefully into a split, her eyes followed Ken, who was dashing up and down in front of the bleachers, handing out flyers urging people to pick Jessica's squad. A glow of love softened her face. *He's really nuts about me,* she thought, wanting to laugh out loud. *And I'm really nuts about him. This whole thing just feels so . . . nice! How did it happen? Why didn't it happen sooner?*

She didn't really want to question it; she was just glad that she and Ken had found each other. *And I suppose I have Elizabeth to thank as much as anyone,* Jessica thought with secret amusement, *for letting Ken go so he'd be free to fall in love with me!*

Just then Mr. Cooper and Coach Schultz, the SVH athletic director, strode onto the basketball court, microphones in hand. "We're just about ready to begin the cheer-off," Coach Schultz announced, his deep, scratchy voice resounding throughout the gym. "We flipped a coin, and Jessica Wakefield's squad will perform first. One more minute, girls, and then you're on!"

Jessica bounced to her feet and quickly gathered her squad around. "So who's nervous?" she asked when they were in a huddle. All seven girls raised their hands. Jessica laughed. "That's OK. Being a little nervous gets the adrenaline flowing and keeps you on your toes."

"I'm worried about performing on the hard

floor," confessed Jade. "We've only practiced outside on the grass. This surface feels different!"

"It's not that different," Jessica assured her. "You'll be fine, all of you." She flashed a wide, encouraging smile. "Now, I'm counting on you to get me to regionals, OK?"

The squad closed in tight for a group hug. Then they clapped their hands loudly, gave a shout, picked up their pom-poms, and trotted into position facing the bleachers.

As they waited for their music to start, Jessica felt her heartbeat quicken in anticipation. Ken was sitting front and center, a red-and-white banner in his hand; he caught her eye and winked. A surge of adrenaline flooded Jessica's veins, and then the music began.

For a few minutes Jessica wasn't aware of anything or anyone other than the seven girls she was performing with—it was as if Mr. Cooper and Coach Schultz, Heather's squad, and the hundreds of students packed in the bleachers ceased to exist. The only thing she could hear or feel was the music and her body responding to it; her entire being was concentrated on the act of keeping in sync with her squad and performing her arm movements, footwork, and jumps with flair and precision.

The routine ended with each girl performing her most dramatic and polished jump combination, and then they piled themselves into a pyramid. As Jessica and Lila boosted Jade to the top and then took their places at the side to support the girls at the bottom, the crowd leaped to its feet in a standing ovation.

The applause was thunderous; Jessica curtsied, a huge smile lighting up her face. Jade hopped down, followed by Patty and Sara; then all eight girls fell on each other, hugging and laughing. "We did it!" Maria cried.

"Not a single mistake!" exclaimed Lila.

"There's no way Heather can beat that, no way," declared Jessica, her cheeks flushed with triumph. "We're going to regionals, you guys. I'm sure of it!"

The crowd was still shouting and stomping with approval as Jessica and her squad trotted over to the bench. As soon as they sat down, Todd and Ken plied them with towels and bottles of water. Elizabeth took a towel from Todd. As she blotted the perspiration from her forehead, she surreptitiously sneaked a glance at her sister and Ken. Ken was standing behind Jessica, rubbing her shoulders and whispering something in her ear. Jessica's eyes were closed; she leaned into Ken, a blissful smile on her face. *At this moment she has everything she's ever wanted—her life is perfect,* Elizabeth thought, an unaccountable flash of jealousy piercing her heart. *What kind of crummy sister am I? Why can't I be happy for her?*

Coach Schultz was speaking into the microphone again. "That's a pretty enthusiastic response for Jessica's squad," he observed in a hearty tone. "Now, don't wear yourselves out, because there's another very fine cheerleading squad waiting to

134

perform for you. Let me present to you Heather Mallone, Amy Sutton, Jean West, and Annie Whitman!"

If Heather was nervous, it didn't show. Elizabeth sat up straighter; so did Jessica and the rest of her squad. Suddenly, the giddy smiles disappeared. Even Jessica had started chewing her nails. Elizabeth's mouth went dry; she took a slug of water. *We did our very best, but we can't take victory for granted,* she thought, wiping another bead of sweat from her forehead.

The music started, and Heather and her squad launched into a spunky, playful routine, the kind of routine that makes people start tapping their feet and clapping to the beat. They, too, had been busy the previous week; it was an all-new routine, as fresh and original as anything Elizabeth had ever seen. *It's as good as our routine,* she realized, gulping. *Maybe even better.*

And there was no doubt that Heather, Amy, Jean, and Annie were the cream of the old SVH cheerleading crop. No one could kick higher, spin faster, or jump, cartwheel, and flip with more pizzazz. They were athletic, sexy, and sharp. The audience loved them.

Their routine complete, Heather and her squad posed for the crowd, waving like beauty-pageant contestants. A few people threw tissue-wrapped bouquets of flowers. Elizabeth glanced at her twin; Jessica was pale as a ghost.

Chrome Dome Cooper waved for silence. When the crowd simmered down, he cleared his throat. "Ahem. We've seen both squads perform, and if I may say so myself, our high school appears to have a surplus of talent. What show-stopping numbers! Now for the vote."

Elizabeth slid over on the bench so she could squeeze her sister's hand; Jessica's fingers were as cold as ice.

Chrome Dome continued. "Instead of taking a hand count, we're going to ask you to vote with your feet. Those of you who support Jessica's squad, gather over at this bleacher"—he pointed one way—"and those of you voting for Heather's squad, assemble over here. Ready, set, go!"

A rowdy melee ensued, with students scrambling down from one bleacher to race over to the opposite side of the gym. For the first minute or two, it looked as if more people were piling onto Jessica's bleacher. The healthy glow returned to Jessica's complexion; she smiled joyfully. "It's looking good," she whispered excitedly to Elizabeth. "It's looking really good!"

But by the time everyone had settled down again in their new seats, the numbers appeared to have evened out. Elizabeth, Jessica, and the other girls watched with bated breath as Mr. Cooper and Coach Schultz each headed over to one of the bleachers to quickly count heads.

Afterward, the two men met in the middle of the basketball court and exchanged a few words. Elizabeth saw both sets of bushy eyebrows shoot up in disbelief. *It can't be,* she thought.

Shaking his head, Mr. Cooper returned to the

microphone. "The impossible appears to have happened," he informed the crowd. "I counted the exact same number of votes for Jessica's squad as Coach Schultz counted for Heather's. It's a tie!"

Jessica's jaw dropped. "A tie?" she exclaimed incredulously.

"Who will get to go to regionals?" Patty wondered.

"Look!" Elizabeth was pointing toward the center of the court. "Isn't that Mr. Jenkins, the ACA scout?"

Jessica whirled to see. A man had emerged from the audience to join Mr. Cooper and Coach Schultz. "None other," Jessica confirmed, surprised.

"Do you suppose he'll cast the deciding vote?" asked Sandy.

The three men conferred for a moment. Then, beaming, Mr. Cooper presented Mr. Jenkins to the student body. "Mr. Jenkins attended this historic event as an official representative of the American Cheerleading Association," the principal proclaimed, "and as such, he is ready to propose a delightful solution to our difficult dilemma. Mr. Jenkins?"

Mr. Jenkins took the microphone. "I came today prepared to congratulate the winning squad on earning a regionals berth," he said, "and I'm happy to say that despite the tie vote, I can still do that. There's no reason any of this talent should go to waste. Sweet Valley High can compete in regionals if the two teams merge, with Jessica Wakefield and Heather Mallone serving as cocaptains once more. Congratulations, girls! You're all going to regionals!"

Both squads had been paralyzed with suspense. Now they exploded joyfully, dashing across the court to congratulate each other. Annie hugged Maria; Sandy hugged Jean; Amy hugged Elizabeth. After all the animosity and competition, everyone was thrilled to be reunited.

That is, everyone but Jessica and Heather. Jessica hung back, her feet rooted to the floor. On the other side of the basketball court, Heather also was refusing to budge. Even from a distance Jessica could see her archenemy's face contort with fury.

Go to regionals . . . with Heather? Cocaptains again . . . with Heather? *Never!* Jessica thought, her hands tightening into fists. *Never, ever, ever!*

Heather bolted toward the cluster of jumping, laughing cheerleaders; Jessica charged forward as well. She didn't know what Heather was going to say, but she wanted to make sure her team understood in no uncertain terms that a merger was out of the question. Out of the question.

"I'm sorry Mr. Jenkins got your hopes up," Heather growled through clenched teeth as she collared Annie, Amy, and Jean, "because we're not going to regionals. I would rather cheer barefoot on hot coals than cheer with that girl!"

Heather hustled her squad away from Jessica's. Jessica faced her own squad, her eyes flashing

138

sparks. "I'm sorry, too," she said, choking on the words, "but we're not going to regionals, either. I would rather cheer naked in Siberia than cheer with that girl!"

"But, Jessica!" cried Maria. "We've been practicing so hard! It could work if you'd only—"

"I said no, and that's final!" barked Jessica. Blinded by tears of anger and disappointment, she turned her back on her squad and walked away.

The dream of competing at regionals had turned to dust.

Chapter 10

Slowly, the Sweet Valley High gymnasium emptied out. After pronouncing their ultimatums, both Jessica and Heather had stormed off. Mr. Jenkins had long since thrown up his hands and headed home, as had Coach Schultz and Chrome Dome Cooper. Only the members of the two cheerleading squads remained, standing in the middle of the basketball court and staring dejectedly at each other.

"It's not fair," Amy burst out, stamping her foot. "Why should it be up to them to decide if we go to regionals or not?"

"We've all worked too hard to just let it go," Jade agreed, an uncharacteristic intensity in her soft voice.

"I can't believe I spent all that money on cheerleading uniforms for nothing," bemoaned Lila.

"I was dying to go to regionals," confessed

Annie, her green eyes glittering with unshed tears. "I've dreamed of this for years, ever since I first started cheerleading."

Maria put a comforting arm around Annie's shoulder. "We all have," she said sadly.

When Jessica flounced out of the gym in a tantrum, and it became clear that the new cheerleading squad had crashed before it even got off the ground, Elizabeth expected to feel relieved. After all, she hadn't wanted to be a cheerleader; there were other, more important things she could be doing with her free time, like writing for *The Oracle*. But now, to her surprise, she found herself feeling as cheated and disappointed as the rest of the girls.

"You're right," she said. "It's not fair, it's not fair at all. Heather and Jessica are our captains, but that shouldn't give them total control over our destiny. We should all have a say in this—we can't let them get away with being so high-handed!"

"But if Mr. Jenkins says we can only go to regionals if the two squads merge with Jessica and Heather as cocaptains, but Jessica and Heather refuse to be cocaptains . . . where does that leave us?" asked Sandy.

"I'll tell you one thing, I'm going to make Jessica pay me back for these uniforms," Lila was muttering under her breath.

"Maybe if either Jessica or Heather would agree to step down," hypothesized Sara.

"Those two? No way, they're too stubborn," said Amy.

141

"Never in a million years," confirmed Maria.

Sara sighed. "It was just a thought."

Patty turned to Elizabeth. "Liz, you know Jessica better than anyone. Can't you think of a way to work this out?"

Elizabeth frowned, her brow creased with concentration. "There has to be an answer," she agreed. "But what is it?"

Jean heaved a defeated sigh. "It's hopeless," she said mournfully. " 'Bye, everybody. I'm going home."

One by one the cheerleaders gathered up their pom-poms and walked with slumped shoulders and heavy footsteps toward the gym exit. "Just give me some time," Elizabeth called after them. "I know I'll think of something."

There were a couple nods, a few halfhearted waves, but Elizabeth could tell the girls didn't put much faith in the prospect of Elizabeth or anyone coming up with a scheme for reconciling Heather and Jessica.

Maybe Jean's right, maybe it is hopeless, Elizabeth concluded wearily as she climbed into the driver's seat of the Jeep. But even as she entertained this thought just for a second, Elizabeth felt her spine stiffen with protest. The word "hopeless" wasn't part of her vocabulary. She'd always taken pride in finishing what she started; she wasn't a quitter.

"Every problem has a solution," Elizabeth said out loud to herself. That is, every problem except this thing with Ken and Todd. . . .

She backed the Jeep out of the parking space. "This problem has a solution," she corrected herself, "and I'll find out what it is. I'll think of something. . . ."

"What's going on?" Jessica asked suspiciously.

It was the day after the disastrous cheer-off, and in homeroom Elizabeth had mysteriously informed Jessica that the cheerleaders were meeting in the library during lunch period.

"The cheerleaders are having a meeting?" Jessica had squeaked. "But I didn't call it—I don't even officially have a squad anymore . . . wait a minute. Did Heather call it?"

"We called it ourselves," answered Elizabeth. "Both squads together. Everyone except Heather, that is. So be there!"

When Jessica entered the conference room, Elizabeth and the other girls were clustered with their heads close together, whispering. They all looked at her, their expressions not nearly as solemn as Jessica expected. A few of the girls were even smiling. *As if everything's hunky-dory!* Jessica thought. *As if we're going to regionals or something!* "What's going on?" she asked bluntly.

Amy cleared her throat, sounding for all the world like Chrome Dome Cooper. "Ahem. We have an announcement to make," she said in an important tone. "We—the combined cheerleading squads—would like to go to regionals." She lifted a hand before Jessica could protest. "And we want you to be our sole captain."

143

Jessica dropped into a chair, astonished. "The sole captain? But what about . . ."

"Heather has agreed to stay on the squad but to step down as captain," Elizabeth interjected. "It was a tough sell, let me tell you, but finally we made her see that it was in everybody's best interest. After all, you were here first—you have seniority, and by right you should be the one leading Sweet Valley High to regionals."

"You're kidding," Jessica gasped.

"We're dead serious." Lila grinned. "Isn't it great?"

As the news slowly sank into her brain, a smile began to spread across Jessica's face. "Boy, I wish I'd been there to hear Heather resign," she murmured. "I'm the captain. I'm the captain and we're going to regionals!"

"So you'll take responsibility for all of us?" asked Annie.

"Well, I'll tell you the truth." Jessica leaned back in the chair and clasped her hands behind her head, reveling in her newly bestowed power. "I'd be happier if Heather were off the squad altogether."

"We know you don't like her, but you have to admit we need her," said Jean.

"She's done a lot for cheerleading at SVH," Amy chimed in. "Without her talent, her spark, her new ideas, we'd never have caught Mr. Jenkins's eye in the first place."

It was true; Jessica couldn't argue. Reluctantly, she nodded her head. "I guess you're right."

"You really don't know," Elizabeth told her sister, "what a feat it was getting Heather to agree to stay on the squad but not be the captain. I mean, you know how ambitious she is."

Jessica beamed. "And now she's going to be taking orders from me!"

"Don't make her bitter by gloating," Elizabeth advised. "Since you won, you can afford to be generous. At practice this afternoon, two thirty on the atheltic field, let her think she's still calling the shots."

"Sure," agreed Jessica, her manner smug and self-satisfied. "I'll humor her a little."

"This is great," exclaimed Amy, reaching across the table to clasp Jessica's hand. "We'll be cheering together again, Jess. And we're going to regionals!"

As the other girls applauded, Jessica indulged in a little fantasy. She was on stage at regionals, accepting the first-prize trophy, flanked by the rest of her squad . . . including Heather, now just one of the girls. *I'm back on top,* Jessica thought exuberantly, *where I belong!*

At two fifteen all the cheerleaders with the exception of Jessica were gathered outside on the athletic field, waiting for Heather. Nervously, Maria looked at her wristwatch. "What if Heather's late?" she asked. "What if Jessica shows up early? Maybe we should have told her two forty-five instead of two thirty, to give ourselves extra time."

"Don't worry," Elizabeth said soothingly, although she, too, was growing nervous. "We have the situation under control."

"And here comes Heather now," drawled Lila.

Heather strode across the grass toward them, dressed in turquoise bike shorts, a big white T-shirt, and sneakers. She was not smiling. "What's the story?" she asked without preamble. "Who called this practice?"

"We did," said Elizabeth.

Heather cocked an eyebrow at Elizabeth. "You? You're not on my squad."

"Yes, I am," Elizabeth said serenely.

Heather put her hands on her hips and opened her mouth. Amy intervened quickly. "The two squads are combining like Mr. Jenkins suggested," she explained, "so we can go to regionals. And we want you to be our sole captain."

Heather blinked. "Me?"

"You," confirmed Jean. "You're the one who deserves credit for turning the squad around."

"But what about Wakefield?" demanded Heather. She glanced at Elizabeth. "I mean, the other Wakefield."

"She's agreed to step down in favor of your leadership," said Lila. "She'll still be on the squad, of course, but she'll just be a regular member rather than a cocaptain."

Heather shook her long blond hair, amazed. "She really agreed to all this?"

"She's committed to seeing the SVH cheerleaders go as far as they can go," said Elizabeth, "and we finally made her see that this arrangement was the best way to make sure not only that we get to regionals but that we win regionals."

146

A triumphant smile illuminated Heather's face. "Who'd have thought that girl would show so much sense?" she said snidely.

"So you'll do it?" asked Maria. "You'll be our captain?"

Heather tipped her head to one side, considering. "I probably don't need to tell you that I'd be happier if Jessica was off the squad altogether."

Elizabeth exchanged a glance with Amy and they both stifled a giggle. "No, you don't have to tell us that," said Amy. "But you have to admit, we'd be nothing without the new girls Jessica recruited and trained."

"And the new girls won't cheer without Jessica," declared Patty.

"Also, the twin factor will be a big plus at regionals," added Sandy. "Mr. Jenkins was just wild about it."

"Yep, we need Jessica," Amy concluded. "No two ways about it."

"Well . . . OK," said Heather grudgingly. "Jessica stays. But I notice she's late for practice."

Once again Elizabeth had to smother a grin. "Oh, she'll be here any minute now."

"She's probably just a little embarrassed," Amy surmised. "I mean, it was kind of a blow to her pride, giving up the captaincy and all. You probably shouldn't rub her nose in it. Let her think she's still in charge."

Heather nodded knowingly, and this time Elizabeth had to turn away to hide her smile. "We did it!" she whispered, surreptitiously high-fiving Lila. "We fooled them both."

"It was ridiculously easy," Lila whispered back. "I guess we're lucky those two have such huge egos!"

The Wakefields' doorbell rang at about five thirty, and Elizabeth trotted downstairs to answer it. When she saw who was standing on the front step, her cheeks flushed scarlet. "Oh, hi, Ken," she said. "Um, come on in."

"Hey, Liz." Ken stepped in the hall. "Could you tell Jessica I'm here? We're driving up to Las Palmas Canyon for a picnic."

"Oh." Elizabeth pictured her sister and Ken standing above the breathtaking gorge at sunset, their arms around each other. The thought made her sick to her stomach. "Yeah, sure," she choked out, turning to dash back up the stairs. "She'll be right down."

When she got to Jessica's room, though, she heard the shower running. She shouted something to her sister and then slowly returned to the front hallway. "She'll be a few more minutes," she informed Ken. "Uh . . ." She couldn't just leave him standing there in the hall. "I was just about to start dinner. Can I get you something to drink? Iced tea, maybe?"

"That would be great," said Ken, following her to the kitchen.

As soon as they entered the kitchen, Elizabeth realized it wasn't the most neutral place for her and Ken to hang out. *Does he remember?* she wondered, shooting a glance at him out of the corner of her eye as she opened the fridge to remove the pitcher of iced tea. *Does he remember that we were in the kitchen making sub sandwiches for a party at my house the first time we kissed? Does he remember taking the plate from my hand and pulling me outside to the patio where it was dark?*

Her own heart was pounding from the memory, but Ken appeared completely at ease and oblivious. Elizabeth poured two glasses of iced tea, topped them with slivers of lemon, and handed one to Ken. "Jess and I got home only about half an hour ago," she explained, "and I got the first shower. Cheerleading practice ran kind of late."

"I heard all about it from Jess," said Ken. Tipping back his head, he swallowed half the tea in one gulp. Elizabeth caught herself staring at his throat and tore her eyes away. "The two squads have combined and she's the captain. I've never seen her more psyched about anything. But how'd you pull it off?" He smiled. "How'd you handle Heather the Horrible?"

Elizabeth smiled back. "Well . . ." Suddenly she was bursting to tell him the truth. "Do you really want to know?"

Ken nodded. "I'm dying to know."

"It's a bit of a conspiracy," Elizabeth admitted, "and you have to promise not to tell Jessica."

"I promise," said Ken, his eyes bright with curiosity.

"First we met with Jessica, and then we met

with Heather, and . . ." Elizabeth recounted the two cheerleader meetings held earlier that day.

Ken burst out laughing. "You mean Jessica thinks she's the captain and Heather thinks she's the captain, but in reality they're both captains only they don't know it?"

Elizabeth grinned. "Pretty sly, huh?"

Ken shook his head ruefully. "Boy, when Jess finds out . . ."

"She won't find out till regionals, and by then either we'll have won or lost and it won't matter," said Elizabeth. "The point is just to go and show our stuff. After that she and Heather are free to battle it out."

"Liz, Liz," said Ken, clucking his tongue. "Who'd have thought you could be so devious?"

Elizabeth dropped her eyes, smiling. *Don't you remember? Don't you remember when we both had to be devious, when we had to sneak around and tell lies in order to be together, but it was worth it because we couldn't stand to be apart?*

"Ken, I—"

At that instant Jessica breezed into the kitchen, her blond hair still damp from the shower, looking fresh and sexy in sage-colored linen shorts and a crisp white tank top. "Here you are," she said to Ken, hurrying forward to greet him with a big hug and kiss. "Has Liz been telling you what a marvelous cheerleading captain I am?"

"As a matter of fact, yes," said Ken, winking at Elizabeth over Jessica's head. "That's the very topic we were discussing."

150

Jessica linked her arm through Ken's and propelled him toward the door. "See ya later," she said to her sister. Now it was Jessica's turn to wink. "Don't wait up for me, OK?"

Elizabeth waved good-bye. When she was alone, she leaned back against the kitchen counter, sipping her iced tea with a contemplative expression on her face. Her pulse was still racing because of how close she'd come to confessing to Ken that she still had feelings for him. *I'm glad Jess came along when she did,* Elizabeth thought. *At least . . .I think I'm glad.*

Yes, I am glad, she decided a moment later. It was clear that for Ken their romance was long over. Just because she was insanely confused, why make things more complicated for him?

Insanely confused . . . and incredibly attracted. Elizabeth shivered pleasantly, thinking about Ken and how sweet and adorable he was . . . and that wink! *We have a secret again, him and me,* she thought, hugging herself and smiling. The balance of power had shifted again, slightly in her favor this time. *I know something Jessica doesn't know, for a change!*

Chapter 11

"This isn't going to work," Jessica pronounced at Thursday's cheerleading practice. She tossed her ponytail, eyes blazing. "I'm telling you, I'm this close to strangling that girl!"

Jessica had written a new cheer the night before, and she'd just spent fifteen minutes trying to demonstrate it to the other girls on the squad. But every thirty seconds Heather interrupted her to make a criticism or suggest a change.

"She just likes to . . . express her opinion," said Amy, her tone conciliatory.

"That's putting it mildly," snapped Jessica. "It's like she thinks she's still captain or something. She's driving me crazy!"

Amy glanced over her shoulder at where the rest of the squad was standing around on the grass. "Just try to mellow out, OK?" she advised Jessica. "I know you want to give Heather a piece of your mind, but we don't want to drive her off the squad."

"We don't?" said Jessica testily.

Amy gave her friend's ponytail a playful tweak. "Come on. Take a deep breath and count to ten. We only have a couple more practice sessions before regionals on Saturday, and we can't afford to waste time being mad at each other. We already tried that back when we were two separate squads, remember?"

Jessica rolled her eyes, but she did as Amy said. "One, two, three . . ." she grumbled.

Amy patted her on the back. "Good for you, Jess. You really are the stuff that great cheerleading captains are made of."

They strolled back over to the rest of the squad. "OK," Jessica sang out, her voice falsely cheerful. "How 'bout we hold off on that number for a while? Let's run through the routine that Patty and Jade helped me choreograph. It shouldn't take the rest of you—Amy, Jean, Annie, and Heather—long to pick it up."

Practice pom-poms in hand, the girls lined up on the field. Jessica started the tape player. "Now, the first move," she shouted above the music, "is a sideways dance step that goes like this—"

Jessica started to demonstrate the step. All the other girls followed suit . . . with the exception of Heather.

Angrily, Jessica hit the off button on the tape player. "Now what?" she demanded of Heather, who was standing with her feet rooted to the ground and her pom-poms hanging limp at her sides.

"This just seems like the right time to tell you," said Heather in her snottiest tone, "that I don't really like this cheer."

The nerve of this girl! "You don't like this cheer," Jessica repeated in disbelief. "For your information, this cheer almost won us the cheer-off two days ago."

"'Almost' is the key word," declared Heather. "And you can take my word for it, it won't win us the regionals competition."

Jessica folded her arms across her chest. "Oh, really. And why is that?"

"Because of that dance stuff you're so into," said Heather. "There's too much of it."

Jessica glanced at Patty and Jade, her eyebrows elevated as if to say, Can you believe this garbage?

"I don't think there's too much of it," said Patty.

"Well, yeah." Heather laughed harshly. "Because you put it there, right?"

"It adds elegance," Jade spoke up. "And it's just as technically hard as doing athletic jumps—I think the regionals judges will appreciate that."

"Don't count on it." Heather's know-it-all tone made the hairs on Jessica's arms stand on end. "I've been to regionals with the team from my old school—I've won regionals. I've been to state— I've won state. And the judges are traditionalists. They welcome a certain amount of innovation, but they definitely don't favor routines that have been . . . diluted."

"Dance does not dilute the routine!" cried Patty.

"I like it the way it is," agreed Sara.

"Well, I personally think that if Heather says we should change it—" began Jean.

Suddenly all the girls were talking at once. Everyone had an opinion, and everyone's opinion was different. The bickering voices lifted higher and higher. . . .

"Stop it!" Jessica screeched. "Just shut up, would you?"

The rest of the cheerleaders stared at her. "I think . . ." Jessica began.

She was about to say, "I think you should keep your fat mouth shut from now on if you want to cheer on my squad, Heather Mallone!" Instead, after clearing her throat and making a massive effort to suppress her temper, she said, "I think that's enough for today. See you guys back out here tomorrow afternoon."

She walked away quickly, not trusting herself to talk to anyone. As she neared the edge of the field, she saw that Ken had been standing there watching. "Pretty good show, huh?" she greeted him morosely.

"Better than female mud wrestling," Ken joked.

He put his arm around her, and she leaned into him with a frustrated sigh. "I just don't know how we're going to pull things together in time for regionals on Saturday."

"You will."

Jessica looked up at him. "How do you know?"

"Because I just know. I know you and I know what you can do, and you can do this."

"Really? You really think so?"

Ken smiled down into her eyes. "I wouldn't say it if I didn't mean it."

"Oh, Ken," whispered Jessica. Twining her fingers in his hair, she pulled his face close to hers for a kiss. "Just knowing you believe in me makes me feel so much better. It makes me feel like I can do anything."

"So kiss me, then," he whispered as his lips met hers.

Despite the resolution that Elizabeth coaxed from Jessica to be calm and tolerant, Friday afternoon's practice was even worse than Thursday's. Every other sentence out of Heather's mouth began, "At my old school we did it like this," which predictably led to constant bickering with Jessica. And with the larger combined squad of twelve girls, choreographing the routines had become a more complex task.

"I don't have a good feeling about this," Annie said to Elizabeth as they took a water break. Annie rubbed her stomach gingerly. "I think it's giving me an ulcer."

"There's so much tension in the air, you could cut it with a knife," Elizabeth agreed, bending over the water fountain.

"I'm mostly afraid that one of them will get so steamed, she'll yell, 'Look, I'm the captain here so we'll do it my way,' and then the other will say,

'What are you talking about, I'm the captain!' and then the you-know-what will really hit the fan."

Elizabeth laughed as they walked back onto the field. "Can you imagine the explosion? They'd feel the shock waves all the way up in San Francisco!"

Both Heather and Jessica shot Elizabeth and Annie dirty looks as they rejoined the squad. "You just missed a very important demonstration," Jessica said somewhat snappishly. "Next time, if you don't mind, you might wait until the whole squad is dismissed for a water break."

"Well, excuse me," Elizabeth said, trying to lighten Jessica up with a smile. Her sister didn't smile back.

"I think we should practice that kick-lunge-hop-jump combination a few more times," Heather suggested, imperiously waving the girls into position.

"We've run through it about a zillion times already," Jessica disagreed.

"And it's still rough," countered Heather. "They'll laugh us off the stage at regionals if we can't even synchronize our kicks!"

"OK." Jessica and Heather flanked the line of cheerleaders. All twelve girls stood at attention, their practice pom-poms on their hips. "Ready, set, go."

Along with the others Elizabeth swung her right leg skyward, toe pointed. Then she lunged forward, hopped to bring her feet back together, and sprang up into a spread-eagle. Out of the corners of her eyes, she'd been able to see the rest of the squad, and it looked pretty good. But Heather still wasn't satisfied.

157

"Patty, your spread-eagle was about two feet higher than everyone else—this isn't the Olympics gymnastics floor routine. And Sandy, did you ever hear about pointing your toe?" Heather shook her head in disgust. "No wonder I didn't want you on my squad," she grumbled, under her breath but still loud enough to be heard.

Jessica stared at Heather, her mouth hanging open. Tears welled up in Sandy's eyes; she ran over to the water fountain to hide them.

"Sorry," Patty said, her voice tight. "I'll try to be more moderate next time."

"You'd better do more than try," advised Heather. She turned to Maria and gave her the eyeball up and down. "And meanwhile, your jump had no elevation whatsoever. Have you put on a few pounds?"

Maria looked stricken. Her hands went automatically to her slender waist. "I don't think—"

"Would you stop criticizing my squad?" Jessica burst out.

"In case you haven't noticed," Heather retorted, "your squad has supposedly combined with my squad, and that means everyone should be performing to the same high standards, but if your squad can't cut it—"

"We know there are still a lot of rough edges," Elizabeth quickly interjected, before the subject of who was really boss could come up, "and we're trying our best, we really are. Thanks for the feedback, Heather. I think it will help us fine-tune the routine for regionals."

"Well, I don't need to remind you that regionals are tomorrow," Heather said, somewhat less huffily.

"No, you don't need to remind us," said Jessica. "All right, let's shift gears. Everybody partner up and practice your jumps—spot and coach each other."

Elizabeth and Maria moved off to a vacant part of the field and spent a few moments catching their breath and stretching. "That was a close call," Maria remarked, sliding onto the grass in a split and flattening her torso forward on top of her extended leg. Balancing on one foot, Elizabeth bent the other leg at the knee and lifted it behind her, then reached back to grab the ankle. "I have to admit I'm starting to worry. We haven't even decided on which routines to perform at the competition tomorrow!"

"Maybe it would have been better to choose one of the two squads to go to regionals," said Maria. "Then SVH would have had a shot at the trophy. As it is, if we can't even work as a team, what chance do we have of winning?"

Elizabeth couldn't think of a good answer to Maria's question. In silence the two girls resumed practicing their jumps. Elizabeth was intensely aware of Ken, who had stopped at the edge of the field on his way to the locker room to watch the cheerleaders. The possibility that his eyes might rest on her energized Elizabeth to jump to new heights, and when at one point Ken tossed a wave her way and shouted, "Looking good, Liz!" she thought she would split in two from joy.

Just knowing Ken will be in the audience is all the motivation I'll need to perform at my peak tomorrow, Elizabeth thought as she returned Ken's casual wave. *But what about the rest of the squad?*

Jessica glanced over at Ken just in time to see him waving and grinning at Elizabeth. For a moment something about the scene struck her as sinister. It was almost as if, for a split second, the world turned upside down and inside out. Instead of dating Jessica, Ken was dating Elizabeth. They'd gone public with their torrid romance instead of keeping it a secret. Elizabeth had never got back together with Todd; she'd been with Ken all along. . . .

Jessica shook her head. *It didn't happen that way,* she reminded herself as Ken walked across the grass toward her. Jessica smiled at him, her eyes shining with love. *Of course it didn't happen that way! He broke up with Liz, he got over her, and now he's with me. Me and only me.*

Ken swept her up in his arms. The warmth of his embrace almost banished the tiny niggling doubt that had stolen into Jessica's heart. Almost. She just couldn't help thinking about how different things might have been. . . .

"I can't believe you're going to eat that," Ken said Friday night as he and Jessica sat down at one of the small round wrought-iron tables at Casey's

Ice Cream Parlor in the Sweet Valley Mall.

Jessica studied her mountainous double-fudge sundae with whipped cream and nuts. "Three flavors of ice cream," she declared blissfully. "It is sinful!"

"I wanted to give you a treat the night before regionals," said Ken, "fuel you up, but if you eat all that, you'll never get off the ground tomorrow."

Jessica laughed. "Don't worry. I'm so nervous, I'm burning calories like crazy. This'll only last me for about half an hour."

Ken spooned into his own smaller sundae. "You shouldn't be nervous. You're the best there is—you'll knock the socks off the regionals judges."

Jessica beamed at him. "You really think so?"

"I really think so."

Jessica nudged Ken's foot with hers under the table. "I know I'll feel inspired because you'll be there watching me."

Ken nudged her back. "It's about time I had a chance to cheer for you."

For a full minute they smiled into each other's eyes while their ice cream started to melt. Finally Jessica broke the spell. "I can't believe we're so moony!" she said, laughing.

"Yeah, how did this happen?" kidded Ken, pretending to be shocked. "I don't usually get this way over girls."

"But I'm not just any girl," Jessica reminded him playfully.

"No, you're not," he agreed, reaching across the table to put his hand on hers. "You're one in a million."

Jessica opened her mouth, about to make a joke about how she couldn't actually be one in a million since she had an identical twin, but then she stopped herself. *Why bring up the subject of Elizabeth and how much alike we are?* she thought. No, she didn't want Ken thinking about her sister—she wanted Ken thinking about her.

At the same time, since they were having such a lovey-dovey, confessional chat, this did seem like a convenient opportunity to pry a little. . . .

"I really feel close to you," Jessica told Ken, her eyelashes lowered shyly. "I don't think . . . I don't think I've ever liked anyone this much." She giggled, her cheeks turning bright pink. "God, I can't believe I said that!"

Ken squeezed her hand. His eyes were deep with answering emotion. "I'm glad you did," he murmured huskily, "because I feel the same way about you."

"It has happened pretty fast, though, hasn't it?"

Ken nodded. "Maybe it's because we were good friends for a long time first, I mean before we . . . you know."

"So we didn't have to spend a lot of time in that getting-to-know-each-other phase, because we already did."

"Something like that."

"But part of the fun of this is that even though we've been friends for ages, now that we're going out, I'm learning new things about you all the time," said Jessica.

"Like . . ."

162

"Like your favorite flavor of ice cream is mocha chip, and even though everyone thinks you're just a jock, you want to study premed in college, and you arrange your T-shirts by order of color in your dresser drawer, and on at least one occasion you've gone skinny-dipping after dark at Secca Lake."

Ken laughed. "Now, don't let all this top-secret, classified information get around."

"What else should I know about you?" asked Jessica. "Any other deep, dark secrets?"

"Sorry to disappoint you. That T-shirt stuff is about as deep and dark as it gets."

"So there's nothing you want to tell me, about your . . . past," Jessica hinted delicately.

Ken shook his head. "Well, I do have one big regret," he admitted.

"You do?" Jessica leaned forward, her eyes wide. Could this be it? Was he finally going to tell her about Elizabeth?

"Yes." Ken rattled his spoon around in his empty ice-cream dish. "I regret that I didn't realize sooner that all the other nice, fun, pretty girls at Sweet Valley High can't hold a candle to Jessica Wakefield."

Jessica was disappointed that Ken hadn't spilled his guts about Elizabeth, but she couldn't be too disappointed when he said something as incredibly sweet as that. *He's protecting Elizabeth's privacy and reputation—he's so chivalrous!* "Things happen when they're supposed to, you know?" she said softly. "I think we found each other at just the right time."

"I couldn't agree more."

163

Ken slid his chair around the table so he could give Jessica a kiss. She rested her head against his shoulder. "It's funny, I don't feel nervous about tomorrow anymore," she told him.

"That's because you're with the king of visualization," he explained. "And right now I'm visualizing you leading the Sweet Valley High team to victory at regionals!"

"Did I ever tell you," Todd said as he and Elizabeth approached Casey's, "that ice cream the night before a big game is the secret to my success on the court?"

Elizabeth laughed. "Oh, really?"

"During basketball season there's always a carton of fudge swirl in the freezer. Once my dad finished it off and forgot to buy more, so I didn't get my good-luck bowl of ice cream before bed. I missed an easy basket in the last couple seconds of the game, and we lost by one point."

"I never knew you were so superstitious!" Elizabeth put her arm around Todd's waist and tickled him. "And I thought your big secret was wearing your good-luck underwear."

He grinned. "Well, that, too."

The moment they walked into Casey's, the smile faded from Elizabeth's face. Suddenly she wasn't in the mood for ice cream—her appetite had been instantly ruined.

Todd waved to Jessica and Ken. "Hi, you two."

Elizabeth forced herself to smile at them. "Fancy meeting you here."

"Getting some of that good-luck ice cream?" Ken called to Todd.

Todd nodded. "You bet. I'm treating Liz."

Knowing Todd would be disappointed if she told him she didn't want anything, Elizabeth ordered a small dish of strawberry. "That's all?" he asked.

She shrugged. "I'm kind of . . . keyed up. I don't think my stomach can handle more than one scoop."

They snagged the last empty table, which fortunately was on the opposite side of the ice-cream parlor from Jessica and Ken. *Maybe they'll leave soon,* Elizabeth thought. Then she might be able to relax and enjoy Todd's company.

"This really is a big thing, going to regionals," he remarked. "I'm proud of you, Liz."

"Thanks."

"It won't make you nervous, having me there watching?"

"Of course not." She swept the hair back from her forehead and smiled. "It'll be nice knowing there are some friendly faces in the audience."

"There'll be a bunch," Todd promised. "I'm going with Ken and Winston. We wouldn't miss it for the world."

"Well, I hope we don't let you down," she said, glancing sideways at Jessica and Ken. Although they'd long since finished their ice cream, the two didn't appear to be in a hurry to leave. *God, I can't believe they're doing that in public!* thought Elizabeth as her sister and Ken smooched. She

165

counted silently in her head, timing the lip-lock. Ten seconds. Eleven, twelve, thirteen . . .

"You won't let us down," Todd was saying. "Even if you don't win the title—and I'm confident you will, by the way—just to compete in regionals is an honor. You're the first squad from SVH ever to qualify! And you personally have been cheering for only two weeks. It's really an incredible achievement, Liz."

"Uh, yeah," she mumbled, tearing her eyes away from Jessica and Ken. "Thanks."

Todd had other caring, supportive words for her, and Elizabeth tried to look attentive as he spoke. But she couldn't think about cheerleading regionals . . . not when Jessica and Ken were just a few tables away winning the make-out regionals!

Chapter 12

It was a misty gray dawn as the cheerleaders gathered in the parking lot at Sweet Valley High to carpool to Carver City, where the regionals competition was being held. Jessica rubbed her upper arms and stamped her feet; even in a bulky sweatshirt and sweatpants, she felt chilled to the bone. "I don't think I've ever had to wake up this early in my life," she complained. "The sun isn't even up!"

Maria yawned widely. "At least you slept. I was so nervous, I didn't close my eyes all night."

"I slept, but I had this horrible nightmare," said Annie, hugging her sports duffel to her chest. "We went onstage at regionals, and halfway through the routine I realized I was wearing underwear and nothing else!"

Jessica and Maria giggled. "I've had that dream," said Maria, "except usually I'm doing something for the student council, like addressing an all-school assembly, and I step up to the podium in the auditorium and—"

Just then a white Mazda Miata peeled into the parking lot. Heather hopped out, looking well rested and perfectly groomed. "I'm glad everyone was punctual. Are you ready?" she greeted the other girls. Her manner was so chirpy, Jessica wanted to smack her. "Are you psyched?"

The group gave a small cheer. "OK, let's hit the road," suggested Jessica. "Liz and I can take two people in the Jeep."

"There's room in my car, too," offered Patty.

"Whoever's left over can ride with me," said Amy.

The drive to Carver City, about forty-five minutes north of Sweet Valley, seemed to pass in a blink. As Elizabeth pulled into the lot adjacent to the high-school athletic complex, Jessica's whole body started to tremble. "Ohmigod, look at all the cars," she said, her teeth chattering. "The Whitehead Academy van—they always have the sharpest uniforms, not to mention the fact that their coach used to choreograph routines for the state university squad." She spotted another van and gulped. "And Springbrook High. They've won regionals two years in a row! Oh, Liz, let's go back home. We don't have a prayer!"

"We do so," Elizabeth declared, setting the parking brake.

Sandy leaned forward from the backseat to give Jessica's shoulder a squeeze. "It doesn't matter who won regionals last year. What counts is who's the best today."

"And that's going to be us!" Jean chimed in.

The twins, Sandy, and Jean joined the rest of the squad, and together they marched into the gymnasium. A loud, colorful spectacle met their eyes. Heather was the only one who seemed completely calm and unconcerned—the rest of the girls froze in their tracks.

There were girls everywhere. Brightly colored banners marked off the space where each squad would practice; scanning the gym, Jessica spotted Springbrook High, Whitehead Academy, Fort Carroll, Lawrence, Palisades, San Pedro, Ramsbury. Her teeth started chattering again. "I . . . don't . . . think . . . I . . . can . . . go . . . through . . . with . . ."

Elizabeth gave her sister a shove from behind. "There's nothing to be afraid of, silly." She grinned. "We've got an edge, remember? The twin factor!"

As they made their way to a corner of the gym where there was still some floor space, Jessica checked out the competition. The Whitehead Wildcats, already dressed in their black-and-red uniforms, were gathered in a huddle around their famous coach. A few feet beyond them the San Pedro squad launched into a routine with a fireworks explosion of spectacular sequenced jumps. Jessica paused to watch, then wished she hadn't. It only made her more insecure.

We haven't even decided which routines we're going to perform, she thought, hurrying after the rest of the squad. *We're doomed!*

When Jessica caught up to the others, Heather had already stripped off her sweats and was

169

stretching out. After a few minutes of limbering exercises, the Sweet Valley girls formed a circle. "Why don't we warm up with the school-spirit cheer," Jessica suggested, "and then we can work on the dance number, since that's the one that's been giving us trouble."

To her relief Heather just nodded. *She's keeping her place, finally!* Jessica thought.

The girls fanned out, spacing themselves an arm's length apart. "OK," Jessica shouted, "on the count of three, stomp, clap, yell, and then the wave—spread-eagles in sequence starting with Jade on the far left, and then back crunches for the wave going back the other way. Don't let yourself get caught behind—each girl takes off exactly one beat after the girl next to her. Ready? One, two—"

"Wait a minute," Heather interrupted.

Jessica glared at her. "Do you have something to add?"

"I have something to subtract, actually," she said. "Let's scrap the second wave and save our energy for later in the cheer."

"But it doesn't look balanced if you only do it going one way," Jessica argued. "And besides, didn't you see those girls from San Pedro High? We have to start out with something flashy—we can't play it safe if we want to win!"

"It's hardly playing it safe," Heather countered stubbornly. "I don't want to be out of breath when we go into the star formation for our next jump after the 'Rally, Sweet Valley' yell."

"Well, maybe you're not in as good shape as you

think you are, Heather, if you're knocked out after a double wave," Jessica said sarcastically.

"And maybe you don't know anything about winning a regionals competition if you think a double wave is the answer to all our problems," Heather retorted.

Jessica felt something snap in her brain. Suddenly someone was yelling at Heather at the top of her lungs . . . and Jessica recognized her own voice. "What gives you the right to call all the shots, Heather? We don't need your advice—we were doing just fine until you came along!"

"You were getting nowhere until I came along!" Heather shouted back.

Simultaneously both Jessica and Heather threw down their pom-poms. "I've had it!" Jessica exclaimed.

"Forget it, she's impossible!" Heather declared.

Heather started to stomp in the direction of the water fountain; Jessica was ready to head back out to the parking lot and rev up the Jeep for the trip home. Before either girl could take a step, Amy put her thumb and index finger to her lips and let out a piercing whistle.

Jessica and Heather stopped in their tracks and stared at her. "*You've* had it?" Amy said to them. "What about the rest of us? How do you think we feel?"

Elizabeth stepped to Amy's side. "This self-centered showboating has gone on long enough," she asserted sternly.

Lila joined Elizabeth and Amy. "Right. Either

you two shut up and start working together, or you're both off the squad and we're performing without you!"

One by one the rest of the squad lined up behind Lila, Amy, and Elizabeth. "Are you with us?" Amy demanded.

Jessica hung her head. "I'm with you," she muttered, glancing at Heather out of the corner of her eye.

Heather nodded contritely. "Me, too."

"OK," said Elizabeth. "Then let's practice this cheer, once with a single wave and once with the double wave. Then we can decide which feels best."

After they'd performed the routine the second time, Jessica turned to Heather. "I think you're right about the—" she started to say.

Heather had opened her mouth at the same moment. "Maybe the double wave does work—"

They both burst out laughing. It's going to be OK, Jessica thought.

Miraculously, once Heather and Jessica were back on speaking terms, it took only a few minutes to work out the final kinks in their second routine. After cooling off they retreated into the locker room to change into their uniforms, put on makeup, and brush their hair; then they regrouped once more in the gym.

Jessica was reading the printed program; now she checked the clock on the wall. "The first team is about to perform," she said. "Since we go

172

last, let's rest up for a while and watch."

While they'd been practicing, the bleachers had filled up. As the other girls hurried off, Elizabeth paused to scan the crowd, hoping to spot some friends from Sweet Valley High. Just then someone stepped up behind her and slipped his arms around her waist.

Elizabeth let out a startled gasp; the boy was lightly kissing the back of her neck. He was so close, she could smell the fresh, citrusy scent of his aftershave.

"Hey, Jess," Ken whispered into Elizabeth's ear. "There's a meteor shower tonight. How about we take a blanket down to our secluded beach and catch some falling stars to celebrate your regionals victory?"

Elizabeth's first impulse was to push Ken away, tell him that once again he'd made an understandable mistake. They'd laugh about it, and Ken would run ahead to catch up with Jessica. Then another impulse took over. . . .

I'll tell Jessica that Ken mentioned the meteor shower and the beach and then dashed off again before I could tell him he had the wrong twin, Elizabeth decided as she closed her eyes and leaned back against Ken's broad chest. *She'll have her date tonight with Ken, and what she doesn't know won't hurt her. . . .*

"That sounds great," Elizabeth murmured. "What an incentive to win!"

"I have to head home as soon as the competition's over," Ken said, his arms tightening around

173

her, "so here's your victory hug in advance. I'm with you all the way, Jess!"

"Thanks, Ken," Elizabeth whispered.

Ken kissed her on the cheek and then disappeared into the crowd. Elizabeth stood for a moment, one hand lifted to where Ken's lips had touched her skin. When she refocused, she realized that someone was staring at her.

Heather had retraced her steps to hustle along anyone who was lagging. "Come on, Liz," she called sharply. "Lawrence High is already halfway through their first routine!"

Elizabeth scurried after Heather, her face flaming. *Did she see?* she wondered anxiously. *No, she couldn't have. I would've noticed her sooner.* Elizabeth took comfort in this thought, even though she knew it wasn't necessarily true. While Ken's arms were around her, she hadn't been aware of anything; Todd himself could have been standing right in front of her, and she probably wouldn't have noticed!

"Gosh, they're really good," gushed Lila, nervously twisting a strand of her hair. "Did you see the height on that team stag leap?"

"And it was perfectly timed," said Annie, shaking her head. "What a landing—not one girl misstepped."

The Ramsbury Rockets landed their final jumps in the form of a big *R*, held the pose for a moment, and then waved energetically at the audience. The applause was loud and enthusiastic.

"The crowd liked that a lot," said Jessica, biting her fingernails.

"The judges liked it, too." Heather pointed. "See? They're smiling and whispering to each other. I bet they mark Ramsbury even higher than Springbrook!"

A minute or two passed in tense, expectant silence, and then the point total for the Ramsbury squad flashed on the scoreboard. "They've moved into first place!" squealed Amy.

Jessica grabbed Elizabeth's arm for support. "I think I'm going to pass out. I think I'm starting to hyperventilate!"

"You can't pass out, because after the next team it's our turn," Elizabeth said pragmatically. "Just take slow, steady breaths, Jess. Like this. In, out. In, out."

Jessica breathed in and out as instructed. Then she smiled weakly. "I feel better."

Elizabeth patted her on the back. "I think you're going to make it."

"Thanks for being so calm and sensible, Liz." Jessica gave her sister a spontaneous hug. "Where would I be without you?"

"Passed out or hyperventilating," Lila joked.

"Or both," said Amy.

The spotlight was now on the Fort Carroll cheerleaders, the second-to-last squad to perform. The eight girls trotted to the middle of the basketball court, their ponytails bouncing. Half wore flouncy pleated purple skirts with cropped white sweaters, and the other half wore white skirts with purple sweaters. "Cute uniforms," commented Jessica.

"They look sharp," agreed Elizabeth.

The Fort Carroll team performed their musical number first. It was technically strong, but not that original, Jessica was happy to note. Their second routine was more of the same, a traditional fight cheer with lots of stomping and clapping and a smattering of well-executed jump combinations. "Good but not great," Heather pronounced when they were through.

Sure enough, Fort Carroll's point total was slightly lower than Ramsbury's. "Ramsbury's the team to beat," Jessica said.

Heather nodded. "And Sweet Valley's the team to beat them!"

The two girls looked each other straight in the eye. For the first time since she'd met Heather, Jessica didn't hate and resent her; she felt camaraderie and, of all things, trust. *I can count on her,* Jessica thought. *We'll never be best buddies, but when it comes to cheerleading, she's a pro. She'll pull out all the stops—she'll blow the judges away.*

Jessica smiled; Heather grinned. "So," Jessica said to the rest of the squad. "Everybody ready?"

They didn't even have time for one last pep talk. "And now, last but not least, Sweet Valley High!" the announcer boomed.

As she jogged out onto the court with Heather and the other girls and felt the energy pulsing from the audience, Jessica's nervousness melted away, and her love of the limelight asserted itself full force. She smiled broadly, radiating pure joy in the moment. *This is it! We're on!*

They'd opted to start with their shorter school-spirit yell, saving the innovative dance routine for their finale. As she sprang into motion, kicking, swaying, clapping, twirling, jumping, shouting, Jessica was aware of the other girls in the squad, aware that they were watching her out of the corner of their eyes, using her as their guide. She felt her body respond to the demands she made of it—she knew she'd never looked stronger, crisper, more in control.

The regionals audience enjoyed the first routine; they went wild over the second. As the Sweet Valley High squad struck their final pose, Jessica glanced at Heather. Heather was breathing hard, but she was beaming. "We were brilliant!" she mouthed to Jessica.

Pom-poms on their hips, Jessica and the others waited for their score. The judges put their heads together; they conferred for what seemed to Jessica like a year. "We were the best," she murmured to herself. "At least, I think we were. But Ramsbury was awfully good. Maybe we didn't quite cut it. Sara was a teeny bit behind on that last jump. Oh, I can't stand it!"

The judges appeared to have reached a consensus. Clutching each other for support, her teammates stared at the scoreboard; Jessica covered her eyes.

Then the crowd let out a roar of approval; Jessica felt someone grab her and shake her.

177

"We did it!" Lila screeched. "We won!"

The Sweet Valley High squad exploded into the air, tossing their pom-poms and shouting with joy. Jessica grabbed Amy and twirled her around. "Do you see that?" she whooped. "Do you see those scores?"

They quieted down as the judges presented the runners-up trophy to a disappointed but gracious Ramsbury squad. Then it was Sweet Valley's turn. Jessica's heart started pounding as the head judge spoke into the microphone. "And now we're pleased to present the grand-prize trophy to the team that will be representing our region at the State Cheerleading Championships. On behalf of your squad, will Sweet Valley High cocaptains Heather Mallone and Jessica Wakefield please step to the podium?"

Jessica took a step forward and then halted, her mouth falling open. "Cocaptains?" she yelped, shooting an accusing look at Heather. "I thought I was the captain!"

Heather glared back at her. "No, I'm the captain. They told me you agreed to step down."

Jessica shook her head. "They told me *you* agreed to step down!"

The judges and everyone else in the gym were still waiting for Jessica and Heather to accept the trophy. Elizabeth tried to propel her sister forward. "Don't blow it now!" Elizabeth hissed.

Jessica put her hands on her hips, refusing to budge. "Forget it," she fumed. She couldn't believe how badly she'd been duped. "If you want her to be your captain, I quit."

"If you want her to be your captain, I quit," Heather echoed.

Amy stepped forward. "If you two won't agree once and for all to be cocaptains, we all quit," she announced, her voice loud and firm. "Either we all go to state, or none of us goes!"

The rest of the squad nodded, clearly backing Amy in her ultimatum a hundred percent. Reluctantly, Jessica turned to face Heather.

Heather extended her hand. "Truce."

Jessica shook Heather's hand. "Truce."

A moment later the two cocaptains were each holding a handle of the heavy silver trophy while the crowd gave them a standing ovation. Suddenly the reality hit Jessica and she burst into tears of joy. "We won!" she cried, flinging her free arm around her twin sister.

"We won!" Elizabeth agreed, her own eyes shining with the thrill of victory. "We're going to state!"

Chapter 13

"I still can't believe it," sang Jessica, dancing across the kitchen in a giddy circle. She grabbed Elizabeth, whirling her around, too. "We won regionals. It's official—Sweet Valley High cheerleaders are the best!"

"You were great," Elizabeth told her sister truthfully. "It couldn't have happened without you, Jess. All the girls think so."

"Then why did you play that mean trick on me?" asked Jessica, pretending to pout. "Faking me out that I was the only captain, and then doing the same thing to Heather."

"Because we knew it was the only way to keep you both on the squad since you were too stubborn to serve as cocaptains." Elizabeth smiled. "And it worked, didn't it?"

Jessica laughed. "You're right. I guess I can't be too mad about it! And Heather's starting to come around. I'm never going to like that girl, but I can put up with her. At least until we win states and then nationals!"

"That's the spirit!" said Elizabeth as she ripped open a bag of pretzels and offered them to her sister.

Jessica shook her head at the pretzels and then reached for the phone. "I'm going to call Ken and then—"

Elizabeth slapped the heel of her hand to her forehead. "I almost forgot," she exclaimed. "Ken gave me a message for you."

Jessica's eyebrows lifted in surprise. "He did?"

Elizabeth nodded. *Is my face turning red?* she wondered. *Can Jessica tell that Ken held me in his arms and whispered the message in my ear?* "Well, he thought he was talking to you," explained Elizabeth, laughing to hide her discomfort. "He was kind of in a hurry—he didn't realize—"

"Spit it out," Jessica commanded. "What did he say?"

"He said . . ." *Say it: He wants to take you to your private beach and watch the shooting stars.* "He won't be able to see you tonight because he has some family party to go to. But he's really proud of you and he'll call you tomorrow."

Elizabeth regretted the lie as soon as it left her lips, but she couldn't call the words back. They were out there; she'd set the wheels in motion.

"Oh." Jessica's face fell with disappointment. Then it brightened again. "Well, in that case, I guess I'll party at Lila's with the cheerleaders. Her parents are ordering in a ton of great food—Lila's inviting a bunch of people. Want to go with me?"

Elizabeth patted her mouth, faking a huge yawn. "I'm beat—I might just curl up in bed with a book."

"Suit yourself." Jessica grabbed a set of keys off the counter. "Then you won't be needing the Jeep?"

"Nope. It's all yours."

As soon as the door shut behind Jessica, Elizabeth sank back against the counter, her knees buckling. *I can't believe I did that!* she thought, amazed at her own duplicity. But it wasn't what she'd already done that most astonished Elizabeth. It was what she was intending to do.

Picking up the phone, she dialed Todd's number. "Hi, it's me, Liz," she said when he answered. "I'm going to have to cancel our date tonight. I'm so wiped out from regionals—I think I'll just take a long, hot bath and go to bed early. But I'll see you tomorrow, OK?"

After hanging up she sprinted into the hall and up the stairs. Instead of entering her own bedroom, however, she barged into Jessica's, making a beeline for the closet. As usual, Jessica's wardrobe was in total disarray, with clothes lying knee-deep on the closet floor and dangling haphazardly off hangers. *Something casual but sexy*, Elizabeth thought, rummaging through Jessica's blouses and tank tops. *Something that won't get too wrinkled when I'm lying on the sand with Ken. . . .*

After choosing a pair of gauzy white trousers

and a clingy crocheted top, she glanced at her watch to see how much time she had to get ready. Then she laughed out loud. *What a dead give-away!* she thought, quickly unbuckling the leather strap from her wrist.

Because Jessica never wears a watch. And if I want Ken to think I'm Jessica—and that's the only way I'm going to be able to get close to him—I'd better make sure I get every detail just right. . . .

There were no other cars in the parking lot by the beach when Ken's white Toyota pulled in. "Good," he said, shooting a sexy smile at Elizabeth. "Looks like we'll have the ocean and stars all to ourselves, Jess."

A shiver of anticipation chased up Elizabeth's spine. "Good," she echoed, her voice as soft and caressing as the night breeze.

Ken slung the beach blanket over his shoulder. Hand in hand, he and Elizabeth scrambled over the grassy dune. Before them a sliver of sand gleamed like silver in the moonlight; a crescent of foam marked the waterline.

They stood for a moment, drinking in the peaceful, magical scene. Ken's fingers tightened around Elizabeth's; she returned the pressure. *It's been so long,* she thought, her whole body electrified by Ken's touch, *so long since I was with Ken, since I was with any boy but Todd. . . .*

Quickly Elizabeth forced the thought of Todd out of her mind. She didn't want to feel guilty; she wanted to feel good.

Ken spread the blanket on the sand in the shelter of a dune. He sat down, and Elizabeth lowered herself gingerly beside him. Then he settled onto his back, one arm extended so that Elizabeth could rest her head on his shoulder. They lay side by side, their faces to the velvety-black, star-speckled sky. "There's supposed to be a meteor shower tonight," he told her, pointing upwards. "If we look to the northwest."

As if on cue, a tiny bright object streaked across the sky, then fizzled and disappeared. "There!" exclaimed Ken. "Did you see it?"

"Yes!" An instant later another shooting star appeared, and then another. "It's like fireworks!" Elizabeth breathed.

Ken shifted so that he was lying on his side. His other arm went around Elizabeth, pulling her toward him. Suddenly they were face-to-face, so close Elizabeth could feel the heat of Ken's body. Ken brushed the hair back from her face; her heart started to pound. *He's going to kiss me,* she thought, breathless with desire. At last . . .

Elizabeth closed her eyes. Ken's lips found hers; she pressed her body against his, responding eagerly. The kiss grew longer, deeper. . . .

Something was wrong. Elizabeth's dream was coming true: She was kissing Ken Matthews again, something she'd been thinking about night and day for weeks. But somehow it wasn't quite the way she'd remembered it—it wasn't nearly as exciting as her fantasies. She kept kissing Ken, waiting in vain for the familiar fiery passion of old to ignite her soul, but it didn't happen. Instead Elizabeth felt a fuzzy, affectionate warmth overlaid by a sudden, confusing sorrow. *Todd,* she thought. *I miss Todd. I want to be with Todd, not Ken!*

At that moment Ken pulled back from Elizabeth. She could see his eyes searching hers in the moonlight. "Jess?" he asked, puzzled. "No, wait. It's . . . Liz?"

They jumped apart, sitting up. Ken stared at Elizabeth in shock; Elizabeth covered her face with her hands to hide her shame and embarrassment. "I'm so sorry," she said, her voice cracking. "I can't imagine what you must think of me. Oh, God, how could I have . . ."

She started to cry. Ken patted her back gently. "Ssh. Take it easy. You freaked me out for a minute there, but it's OK, Liz. Just tell me what's going on."

Elizabeth tried to collect herself. "It's just . . ." There was nothing for it but to tell Ken the whole horrible truth. "I've been going crazy with jealousy since you and Jessica started dating," Elizabeth confessed, her cheeks stained scarlet with humiliation. "I wanted to be happy for her, but I couldn't, and it made me realize that I had all sorts of feelings for you that I'd never really dealt with—I just shoved them into this deep, secret place in my heart and figured eventually they'd die off. I've just been . . . I haven't enjoyed being with Todd at all for weeks. And so I wanted to find out if I really was still in love with you, and this seemed like the only way, but now I see it was a terrible mistake,

185

and what would Jessica think if she could see us like this, not to mention Todd!"

A fresh spate of tears flooded from Elizabeth's eyes. Ken hugged her against his shoulder, murmuring soothingly. "It's not the end of the world," he said with a laugh. "Really, Liz. We didn't do anything so terrible. We kissed and then we both discovered it was a mistake. Hardly a major sin. And besides"—he held her away so that he could gaze earnestly into her eyes— "since we're playing true confessions, I've got to admit that I didn't get over you right away, either. What drew me to Jessica at first was the fact that she was your identical twin sister. I could almost pretend she was you."

"But . . . but you love Jessica," Elizabeth whispered.

Ken nodded. "I do. It didn't take long to figure out that I didn't want to pretend, that what I like best about Jess are the qualities that make her uniquely her. She's the Wakefield for me. Which isn't to say that I don't have fond memories of my time with you," Ken hurried to add, "even though the circumstances were kind of painful."

Elizabeth drew in a long breath, then let it out in a heartfelt sigh. "Boy," she said, brushing the tears from her cheeks. "I really made a fool of myself, huh? Throwing myself at you like that—I feel like such an idiot!"

"You shouldn't," insisted Ken. In the moonlight she could see him smile. "If anything, I'm flattered."

"So we can still be friends?"

Ken found Elizabeth's hand and gave it a firm squeeze. "Of course. The best of friends, always. You're a really special person, Liz."

Ken gave her a swift hug and then they hopped to their feet. Elizabeth almost floated back to the car, she felt so lighthearted with relief. *I'm not in love with Ken!* she thought happily. *I was just delirious, dumb, dizzy. Todd's the one for me—always has been, always will be.* Now she did feel something spark in her soul . . . the rekindling of her love for Todd. She could hardly wait to be back in his arms again.

"Great party, Li," said Amy as she filled her plate with Chinese food at the buffet table set up on the patio next to the Fowler Crest swimming pool.

"Don't I always throw great parties?" Lila snapped her fingers to the beat of the rock music blasting from the outdoor speakers. "I mean, can you even imagine uttering the words, 'Mediocre party, Li'?"

Jessica laughed. "You get extra points this time for spontaneity."

Lila smiled as she looked around the backyard, which was decorated with multicolored balloons, mounds of fresh flowers, and an enormous banner reading "Congratulations, SVH Cheerleaders!" "To tell you the truth," she confided, "it wasn't that spontaneous. Mom and Dad figured we'd need a party whether we won or lost. I think if you turn the banner over, it says, 'Sorry you blew it' or something like that."

Using tongs, Jessica placed a plump egg roll on her plate. She was spooning out sweet-and-sour and hot-mustard sauces when Heather strolled up.

"Hi, Jess," Heather said in her usual la-di-da tone.

Jessica's jaw tightened. *No, I'm never going to like this girl,* she thought, *but I have to be nice.* She smiled stiffly. "Hi, Heather. Having a good time?"

"Oh, sure," said Heather. "Although, I must say, I'm so used to winning competitions that I take it a little bit for granted, you know?"

"Umm," murmured Jessica, resisting the urge to give Heather a pinch. *Be nice, be nice!*

"So where's your sister?" Heather asked as she picked up a plate from the buffet.

"I guess she didn't feel like partying," said Jessica. "She's probably doing something truly exciting, like reading in bed."

"Hmm. Or maybe she's out with that adorable blond boy, Ken the quarterback."

"Ken is my boyfriend," Jessica corrected Heather. "Liz goes out with that adorable brown-haired boy, Todd the basketball player."

Heather raised her eyebrows. "Oh, really? But I could have sworn I saw Ken and Liz . . ." The sentence trailed off suggestively. "Maybe it wasn't the way it looked," she concluded.

Jessica stared at Heather. Then she dropped her plate on the buffet table with a clatter. "Excuse me," she mumbled. "I need to make a phone call."

Heather was smiling as Jessica took off across the patio. Dozens of questions raced through Jessica's mind, but she wasn't about to ask Heather and give her the pleasure of realizing she'd caught her off guard. She saw them . . . where? Doing what? Jessica wondered. "Maybe it wasn't the way it looked. . . ." well, what did it look like?

Charging through the French doors, she hurried to the nearest telephone. She dialed her own home number, praying that Elizabeth would answer quickly. *If she's reading in bed, she should pick it up by the second or third ring,* Jessica thought. Even if she's in the bathroom, she'd get it by the fourth or fifth. The phone rang six times, and then the answering machine picked up. "Sorry we're not able to take your call right now, but if you leave your name and number after the tone . . ."

Jessica slammed down the receiver. "Where is she?" she asked out loud.

Todd. Yes, maybe the answer was that simple. Jessica dialed Todd's number. "Oh, Todd, you're home," she said when he answered the phone. "It's Jessica. Is Liz over at your house by any chance?"

"No," said Todd. Jessica could hear the drone of an action movie in the background. "She said she was tired and wanted to go to bed early. Is something wrong?"

"Oh." Jessica chewed her lip. "No, I was just going to try to talk her into coming over to the party at Lila's. I just assumed she'd be with you— I'll try my house. Thanks."

189

So Liz is out, but not with Todd, surmised Jessica as she raced through the marble hall of Fowler Crest and out the front door.

By the time she got home, she'd decided that there was nothing ominous about Elizabeth's not answering the phone. She was probably in the bathtub, running water, and didn't hear it, or else she'd turned off the ringer so she could sleep. *Don't be so paranoid!* Jessica let herself into the house and ran up the stairs two at a time. "Liz?" she called. "Are you there?"

Her sister's bedroom door was open a crack and the light was out. Jessica pushed the door open, reaching for the switch. The light blinked on, revealing a neatly made bed—the room was empty.

"And she's not in the bathroom," Jessica murmured as she cut through it to her own room. "And she wasn't downstairs, so where . . ."

Her eyes came to rest on her closet. The louvered doors were open, which wasn't unusual. But for some reason Jessica suddenly felt a strong hunch. *Liz was in here. She took something from my closet!*

It took her only a second to determine what was missing: her favorite new pants and top, which she'd hung up carefully, not wanting them to get crumpled like the rest of her clothes. Jessica stood in front of her closet, an empty hanger clutched in her hand. *Elizabeth lied to both me and Todd, and then she went somewhere wearing one of my outfits . . . why?*

Suddenly Jessica remembered the message

Elizabeth had given her from Ken. "He couldn't go out with me tonight because he had other plans," Jessica murmured. Her heart contracted into a small, scared fist. "With his family, supposedly. But what if he's really out with . . ."

She couldn't bring herself to voice her suspicion aloud, but the more she thought about it, the more she was convinced that it was true. Hadn't Elizabeth vowed to get Jessica back for blackmailing her into joining the cheerleading squad?

A picture flashed into Jessica's brain, of Elizabeth and Ken talking and laughing in the kitchen the other day when Jessica had walked in. *As if they had some private joke,* thought Jessica. They certainly didn't seem to feel awkward around each other because of what had happened between them in the past. But, of course, they wouldn't feel awkward if they'd gotten involved again in the present, if all that thwarted passion Elizabeth had written about in her diary had come back to life!

"I can't believe she did this to me," Jessica sobbed, tears streaming down her face. "My own twin sister. Pretending to be happy for me when the whole time she was just waiting for a chance to steal Ken back!"

"I feel so much better having cleared things up with you," Elizabeth told Ken as they drove back to Sweet Valley, "but I'm still going to feel guilty about Todd's not knowing."

"Maybe it's time to tell him," said Ken. "I bet

we end up laughing about it—it all happened so long ago, it's just no big deal. And I'll tell Jessica, too."

"Actually, you don't need to do that," said Elizabeth. "She found out."

"You're kidding!" Ken looked at her, surprised. "You told her?"

Elizabeth made a wry face. "Not exactly. She read my diary."

Ken burst out laughing. "Sounds like Jess, all right. So, was she upset? I can't believe she didn't mention it to me!"

"A little shocked, but no, I wouldn't say she was upset." Magnanimously, Elizabeth decided not to tell Ken about the blackmailing angle. "I guess she doesn't view me as a romantic threat."

"Tell you what," said Ken. "Let's go over to Todd's right now. We can get this off our chests once and for all. Won't that feel good?"

Elizabeth nodded. "I suppose I'll have to tell him about tonight's fiasco, too."

Ken shot her a conspiratorial glance. "We could edit the transcript a little."

She laughed. "OK. You're right. Let's get it over with!"

Ken turned the Toyota onto Country Club Drive in the elegant hill section of Sweet Valley. Elizabeth hurriedly practiced her speech to Todd in her head. *I've been meaning to tell you . . . couldn't get up the courage . . . confused, lonely, but never stopped caring for you . . .*

They drove down the Wilkinses' long, winding

driveway. Then Ken let out an exclamation, jolting Elizabeth from her thoughts. "The Jeep! What the . . ."

Elizabeth stared. Sure enough, a familiar white Jeep was parked in front of the house. "Jessica must be here," she said, her forehead crinkling. "I can't imagine why. Unless . . ."

Ken turned to her. "Unless . . . what?"

Instead of answering Elizabeth sprang out of the car and hurried to the front step, Ken close at her heels. *No,* she thought, her hand trembling as she rang the bell. *She promised she wouldn't tell him. Unless somehow she found out about my twin switch tonight. . . .*

Ken joined Elizabeth as the front door swung open to reveal Todd and Jessica standing side by side. Immediately Elizabeth knew that her worst fears had been realized. Jessica's face was teary and vengeful; Todd was pale, stunned.

And Jessica was holding Elizabeth's diary clutched to her chest.

"You didn't," Elizabeth gasped.

"I didn't do anything," cried Jessica. "It was you, Liz!"

The two mismatched couples stared at each other. Ken hung his head, stricken with guilt. Elizabeth forced herself to meet Todd's eyes, then looked away when she saw the ocean of hurt there. Hurt that she herself had inflicted.

"What have I done?" she whispered, her own eyes filling with bitter tears. "What have I done?"

❖   ❖   ❖

"Look, Wilkins, Jessica. We can explain," Ken said.

"I bet," snarled Todd.

Jessica took a step forward, her eyes on Ken's face; Todd, meanwhile, retreated into the hall. After one last agonized glance at Elizabeth, he slammed the door with all his might.

The sound echoed throughout the quiet night. Elizabeth jumped as if she'd been shot, her hand going to her heart. Then she turned on her heel and ran, blinded by tears, toward the Jeep.

Jessica and Ken were left alone. She stood with her arms folded, her shoulders shaking with suppressed sobs. "Jessica." Ken stretched out a hand toward her. "It's OK. Please don't—"

"Get away from me!" she cried. "Don't touch me. Don't come near me!"

"But we have to talk," he said, his voice vibrating with emotion. "You have to give me a chance to—"

"To what?" She stared at him through a wild tangle of blond hair. "To tell me more lies?" She pointed toward the Jeep. "There's the girl you really love—the one you never stopped loving. Why don't you go to her?"

"No," Ken said hoarsely. "Jessica, it's you I—"

"Stop," she sobbed, covering her ears. "I won't listen. I can't trust you or believe you. And I wanted to, I really did. I loved . . ."

Ken reached for her again. Whirling, Jessica ran away from him into the dark night.

The happiest day of her life had turned into a

waking nightmare. Elizabeth had exacted her revenge for being blackmailed onto the squad. Jessica's dream of winning regionals had come true, but the price was too high. . . . It had cost her the boy she loved.

Don't miss Sweet Valley High #114: "V" FOR VICTORY, the last book in this sensational three-part mini-series.

Bantam Books in the Sweet Valley High series
Ask your bookseller for the books you have missed

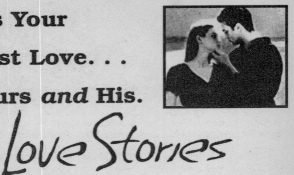

Your friends at Sweet Valley
High have had their world
turned upside down!

Meet one person with a power
so evil, so dangerous, that it
could destroy the entire world
of Sweet Valley!

A Night to Remember, the book that starts it all, is followed
by a six book series filled with romance, drama and suspense.

♡ 29309-5 A NIGHT TO REMEMBER (Magna Edition) ..$3.99/4.99 Can.
♡ 29852-6 THE MORNING AFTER #95 ....$3.50/4.50 Can.
♡ 29853-4 THE ARREST #96 ....$3.50/4.50 Can.
♡ 29854-2 THE VERDICT #97 ....$3.50/4.50 Can.
♡ 29855-0 THE WEDDING #98 ....$3.50/4.50 Can.
♡ 29856-9 BEWARE THE BABYSITTER #99 ....$3.50/4.50 Can.
♡ 29857-7 THE EVIL TWIN #100 ....$3.99/4.99 Can.

Bantam Doubleday Dell
Books for Young Readers

Bantam Doubleday Dell
BFYR 20
2451 South Wolf Road
Des Plaines, IL 60018

Please send the items I have checked above. I am enclosing
$_____ (please add $2.50 to cover postage and handling).
Send check or money order, no cash or C.O.D.s please.

Name _____

Address _____

City _____ State _____ Zip _____

BFYR 20 1/94

Please allow four to six weeks for delivery.
Prices and availability subject to change without notice.

Life after high school gets even *Sweeter!*

Jessica and Elizabeth are now freshmen at Sweet Valley University, where the motto is: Welcome to college — welcome to freedom!

Don't miss any of the books in this fabulous new series.

♥ College Girls #1	0-553-56308-4	$3.50/$4.50 Can.
♥ Love, Lies and Jessica Wakefield #2	0-553-56306-8	$3.50/$4.50 Can.
♥ What Your Parents Don't Know #3	0-553-56307-6	$3.50/$4.50 Can.
♥ Anything for Love #4	0-553-56311-4	$3.50/$4.50 Can.
♥ A Married Woman #5	0-553-56309-2	$3.50/$4.50 Can.
♥ The Love of Her Life #6	0-553-56310-6	$3.50/$4.50 Can.

Bantam Doubleday Dell
Books for Young Readers

Bantam Doubleday Dell
Dept. SVU 12
2451 South Wolf Road
Des Plaines, IL 60018

Please send the items I have checked above. I am enclosing $_____ (please add $2.50 to cover postage and handling). Send check or money order, no cash or C.O.D.s please.

Name _____

Address _____

City _____ State _____ Zip _____

Please allow four to six weeks for delivery.
Prices and availability subject to change without notice.   SVU 12 4/94